I0670787

RACHEL'S FAVORITE VILLAIN

Durango Street Theatre – Book 8

Emily Mims

ALSO BY EMILY MIMS

Durango Street Theatre
Vivi's Leading Man
Maggie's Starring Role
Wade's Dangerous Debut
Jessica's Hero
Letti's Second Act
Cameron Unscripted
Miranda Rewritten

The Smoky Blues
Mist
Smoke
Evergreen
Indigo
Emerald
Mistletoe
Violet
Ruby
Amethyst
Noelle

The Texas Hill Country
Solomon's Choice
After the Heartbreak
A Gift of Trust
Daughter of Valor
Welcome Home
Unexpected Assets
Never and Always
A Gift of Hope

Once, Again

Other Romances
Season of Enchantment
A Dangerous Attraction
For the Thrill of It All

www.BOROUGHSPUBLISHINGGROUP.com

RACHEL'S FAVORITE VILLAIN
Copyright © 2021 Emily Wright Mims

ISBN 978-1-957295-00-8

To all the men and women who have paid their price to society and are now making their way back into a world much different than the one they left. To every one of you:
Good luck and God bless.

ACKNOWLEDGMENTS

As always, this book was not written in a vacuum. Many thanks to beta reader Roy Bartels and the editorial team at Boroughs publishing (especially Michelle) for their thoughts, comments, corrections, and suggestions.

On this, the tenth anniversary of Boroughs Publishing Group, I am so grateful and proud to be a part of a wonderful publishing company that affords me, and every other Boroughs author, the opportunity to tell our unique and varied stories to the world.

RACHEL'S FAVORITE VILLAIN

CHAPTER ONE

Rachel

Rachel stood with her feet planted apart and both hands on the Glock 19 nine-millimeter Luger, her eyes on the paper bullseye a hundred yards away. She ignored the movement behind her and the gunfire from the nearby shooting lanes separated from her by thick plexiglass shields. Slowly and carefully, as she had been taught, she gently squeezed the trigger. A slight smile curved her lips as the bullet tore through the bullseye.

The way it always was when she imagined herself shooting her father's murderer.

Which she would never, *ever* do for real. Her father had taught her better. But she could certainly pretend.

She ejected the spent shell and resumed position, putting four more bullet holes in the center and one slightly left of the target before she stepped back, pleased and a little relieved. Thanks to the pandemic, and then a busy schedule at the theater, it'd been forever since she'd been to target practice. She had been afraid her skills had deteriorated. If she could put five out of six holes in the bullseye, clearly her shooting hadn't suffered too much.

But she could do better.

After all, she was taking down a killer.

She glanced at the target to the immediate left of hers. Hot damn, Owen hadn't lost it either. And he was shooting with only one eye. Her admiration ramped up even more for the medically retired cop with the scarred face and velvet singing voice.

To her right, his husband Wade was doing a fair-to-middling job with his new deer rifle. He'd nailed three of his shots, but three were off by an inch or so. She shrugged. Maybe not perfect, but he could still bring down a white-tailed buck.

She hit the button and her target advanced until she could take it down. She hung a new target and reloaded the pistol. Three more sheets were obliterated before she was satisfied. She unhooked the last one and put her pistol and unused ammo back in the hand-crafted leather gun case her mother had given her for Christmas.

She waited until she was in the lobby to take off her earmuffs and safety goggles. Owen and Wade joined her after stopping to greet a few of Owen's former colleagues from his SAPD days. "You shoot every bit as well as your daddy did," he said. "Raymond would be damned proud."

"Thanks. It means a lot coming from you." She put her earmuffs in her target practice duffel. "Sometimes I wonder if I should've followed him into law enforcement instead of theater."

"No way," Wade said as he packed away the rifle. "You bring too much to the Durango to think you belong anywhere else. You have to be in a theater somewhere."

"Aww, that's sweet. Speaking of the theater, I need to get my butt over there. I scheduled a rehearsal this afternoon and a couple of the actors had to go out of their way to line-up babysitters, like Letti and Kevin."

"Totally true. Uncle Wade and Uncle Owen have Miss Everly. Uncle Owen needs his exercise and he'll get it chasing her. Keeps him trim and sexy like that young stud Letti married." Wade's eyes danced. He and Owen frequently babysat for Owen's ex and her young husband.

"Uncle Owen enjoys every minute with her. Then he can hand her back and go home to his own young stud," Owen said cheerfully.

"When are you and your young stud going to grace our stage again?" she asked as they left the building.

"Don't know," Wade said. "What can you tempt us with?"

Rachel took a deep breath. "If I tell you this, it goes no further." They both nodded. "Josh and I are in negotiations for *Kinky Boots.*"

Their eyes lit up. "But it's a long shot for a community theater. Don't get your hopes up."

"And if *Kinky Boots* falls through?" Wade asked.

"*Priscilla, Queen of the Desert*."

"Which would also be awesome," Owen said.

Wade nodded. "Those two would be a dream."

"They would," she agreed.

Wade and Owen each gave her a one-armed hug. "Be seeing you at the theater... Soon," Owen assured her.

They headed to Wade's pickup and Rachel to her brand new bright blue Dodge Charger, chosen in part for the horses under the hood and in part because it had a backseat large enough to cart around *Abuela* Castillo and Granny Washington.

The balmy October breeze, a welcome change from seven months of Texas heat, reminded her that the clock was ticking on their production of *The Addams Family*. Tech week wasn't far away, and they would open the Friday after Thanksgiving for their Holiday Season, one of the three productions she would direct this year as the Durango's artistic director.

She resisted the temptation to open up the engine on the expressway, limiting herself to a handful of miles over the speed limit. In a few minutes, she had crossed a significant portion of the sprawling city and was pulling into the parking lot behind the Durango. Between Academy classes and the adults rehearsing *Addams Family,* most of the parking places close to the building were already taken, and it was a choice between hiking across the lot or parking next to a dilapidated old pickup. She curled her lip as she pulled into the space next to the pickup and slammed her car door a little harder than she had to, turning her nose into the air as she stalked toward the back door.

The truck wasn't the problem. There were plenty of rundown vehicles in the lot. The owner of the truck was the problem.

Blowing off her annoyance, she made her way through the rabbit warren of dressing rooms and rehearsal halls to her office. Josh and

Maggie's office doors were closed and the lights were off. They were probably enjoying the sunny Saturday afternoon.

She dumped her handbag and ducked across the hall to the big rehearsal room where the cast was gathering. Letti and Kevin hadn't arrived yet, but Academy student Pepe Walsh, playing Pugsley, and Sasha Fontenot, the actress playing Wednesday, were waiting along with Eric Benavides, who was gracing the stage as Gomez. She was about to put them to work on a scene when the front door flew open and her sister Amy ran in, breathless as usual. "Am I late?" she demanded as she skidded into the rehearsal room, her long box braids bouncing with every step.

"Nah, half the cast's not here yet." Rachel plopped down in a chair and motioned for Amy to join her. "Did you get hold of *Abuela* or Granny about Mom's birthday party?"

"I did. Granny's on board, of course, and will be bringing the cake. *Abuela*'s 'not sure.'" Amy made air-quotes.

"Is she ever? You know as well as I do that she'll be there. If for no other reason than to sample Granny's latest dessert so she can go home and try to one-up her at Thanksgiving." Rachel snickered. "Sometimes their rivalry is a pain in the ass, but we sure get a lot of good food out of it."

"Speaking of, what do you want to serve at the party?" Amy asked.

"Hit me with some ideas."

Amy had a smile on her face as she tossed out some tasty menu choices. It was about time, Rachel thought as she noted Amy's enthusiasm. Her older sister's life had sucked big time for the last few years, with a string of loser boyfriends and the loss of a mid-level administrative job with the city. But this year things had finally taken a turn for the better. Amy had finally, *finally* sworn off men until a decent one came along, and she had landed an excellent job in the personnel department of a major department store chain. Along with their sister Felicia, who worked as a high-ranking civilian contractor at Fort Sam and was hardly ever home, they rented a lovely midcentury modern a few blocks from the base entrance and they both were driving brand-spanking new cars. Life was incredibly good for the Castillo sisters.

Rachel was grateful from the bottom of her heart.

She was about stand up and call the actors together when Amy laid a hand on her arm. "I didn't want to say anything, but I don't want you to be blindsided if he shows up so I guess I better. Leshawn texted me this morning. He wants to see me."

Rachel froze, her mellow mood evaporating. Leshawn Hayes had been one of Amy's worst choices in a field of total losers. He'd treated Amy like shit, expecting her to put him up at her place for free despite the perpetual wad of money in his pocket. Rachel had figured out early on the money was obtained illegally, but it took his arrest for dealing for Amy to finally snap to and admit the truth about him. He'd been sent to prison three years ago for what was supposed to be a seven-year sentence. As far as Rachel was concerned, he could stay there forever.

"Well, shit. Does this mean he's out?"

"Released last week, according to his text."

Rachel's eyes narrowed. "Please tell me you didn't text him back."

"I haven't yet."

"Amy."

"I'm trying to figure out how to tell him to fuck off. I'm not interested," Amy snapped.

Rachel raised her eyebrow. "How about 'Fuck off, I'm not interested'?"

"I don't know if it would work. He would think I was playing hard to get."

"You need to do something. The last thing you need in your life is Leshawn Hayes or any of his minions."

"You think I don't agree? I've sworn off him and every other man out there like him. I don't know how I can convince him he needs to go away."

"Turn him down and keep at it until he gets the message." Rachel looked up as Letti and Kevin walked in. "Looks like everyone's here. Time to get to work."

Rachel divided the cast and had them rehearsing three scenes at once. The two who were creating magic were Eric and Amy. Gomez and Morticia were coming to life. Which had Rachel wanting to jump for joy.

At the beginning of rehearsal, she'd wondered if she'd done the right thing in casting them together. Eric was young to be playing Gomez. And while Amy was a beautiful woman, with a knock 'em dead figure and a face that stopped traffic, she was thirty-five and looked every day of it. But damn, if they weren't wonderful together, playing off one another with perfect timing and the right combination of pathos and tongue-in-cheek.

Rachel turned her head at the sound of masculine footsteps in the hall and caught a glimpse of the man as he disappeared into the workroom at the end of the hall. Her lips tightened and she turned her head away.

It was a shame all of Josh and Cameron's choices lately hadn't been as spot on as Eric.

One of their choices had been seriously crappy.

She worked the cast for three hours and thanked them profusely at the end. "Y'all are the absolute best," she enthused to her tired but smiling cast. "Now, go have a wonderful evening. You've earned it."

They scattered in every direction. She unlocked her office and sat down for a few minutes. She had nothing that couldn't wait until Monday, but if she spent a few minutes organizing things now, Monday morning would go much more smoothly. Besides, she had no plans for the evening. Her mother and stepfather, who lived in Houston, weren't coming in like they frequently did on the weekend, and Amy was headed out for an evening with some old friends from high school. Rachel supposed she could hang around the theater and go to Thirties with the *Beauty and the Beast* cast after the show, but she didn't feel like waiting around, making small talk, and ignoring the inevitable comments about why a woman as beautiful as she was didn't have a hot date on Saturday night.

It never seemed to occur to anyone that maybe she didn't have a date because she didn't want one.

She shook her head and answered the last email in her inbox. It wasn't because she didn't like men. She liked them fine. Nice ones. Unlike Amy, Rachel was particular when it came to the men she chose to date. Too particular, according to her mother. Downright persnickety, according to Amy.

"They don't have to be fucking perfect to be worth your time," Amy said when she'd broken up with her last boyfriend, a teacher who'd acted in a couple of Durango productions. "I know my standards are too low," she'd continued when Rachel sputtered an objection. "But yours are so damned high, no man will ever measure up." She'd lowered her voice and put her arm around Rachel's shoulders. "There was only one Raymond Castillo and he's gone now. You're never gonna find a man who measures up to Daddy. You may as well stop trying. Even Mom gave up. Harold's a good man and treats her well, but he's not the man Daddy was and never will be."

If only it were so easy.

She finished the email, shut down her computer, and was about to leave when she heard footsteps coming down the hall. She tensed, hoping it was someone here early for the production this evening and not who she thought it was. But her hopes were dashed when Harlan Burke stuck his head in her office door. "Do you have a minute? I have something I need to run by you."

Her first impulse was to turn him down. Harlan, the new set designer, was the last person she wanted to deal with this afternoon. She had been vociferous in her objections when they'd hired him last month. She'd been appalled when Josh and Cameron had taken him on and she hadn't hesitated to say so. "What do you mean, you're hiring an ex-con?" she'd demanded. "Why would you want to hire someone like him?"

"Because he's really good at what he does and we need him," Josh had said none too patiently.

"We don't need to hire him," she'd snapped. "There are plenty of other carpenters we could find who'd do as good as job as he would."

"No, there aren't. We're not looking for a carpenter, we're looking for a set designer," he'd argued. "Cameron and I went over to the senior center and checked out his work. He's excellent. Phenomenal. We won't find anybody any better than he is."

"I don't care. We don't need somebody like *him* in the theater. Not with his past. There will be hell to pay when the Academy parents find out."

"His past won't make a bit of difference when it comes to doing his job and he will have no occasion to interface with the kids. Besides, he's an old friend of Miguel's. You remember. Our benefactor Miguel. The one who rents this place to us for a dollar a year. The one who's called in a favor and asked us to hire him. So, we hired him."

Over her objections. Harlan had come to work the following Monday dressed in brand-new work clothes, wearing his wariness like another shirt. She'd tried to veil her contempt, but it was all she could do to be civil, and from the coldness in his eyes, she could tell she'd failed miserably.

Since Josh, Cameron, and Maggie didn't seem to have a problem with him being a criminal, they could be the ones to welcome him into the fold. Which they did, with a graciousness she found irritating, but that Harlan seemed to appreciate. She had to admit he'd proven to be a hard worker and was good at his job. With powerful muscles in his arms and shoulders, he had the strength to handle the huge pieces of plywood he used to create the sets.

His first project had been to finish the *Beauty and the Beast* set, and then Josh had put him to work turning an unused space upstairs into more storage. He'd done a wonderful job of both of those projects, but Rachel refused to be impressed. She'd see what the

Addams Family sets looked like before she gave his work a thumbs-up.

His work might earn her seal of approval, but Harlan Burke the ex-con never would.

"I have a few minutes." She gestured to a chair and said nothing more.

He sat in the chair she indicated. His gaze flicked over her face and down her body to where it disappeared behind her desk. On the surface his appraisal might seem casual. But she knew enough about how a man looked at a woman to make her wonder if he was attracted to her.

Damn. She hoped not. That was the last thing she wanted.

She couldn't be attracted to him, even though he had a certain subtle sex appeal.

She glanced at him and then away. He did appeal to her, at least a little. He wasn't particularly tall, maybe a couple of inches taller than her five-eight, but he was well built with strength in his arms and legs and chest.

He was pale in a way that spoke of almost no time outdoors, which was understandable given he'd spent most of the last seven years in a prison cell. His ash brown hair appeared to be growing out, and continually flopped in his face. Hazel eyes stared out at the world from a craggy face with high cheekbones, thin, unsmiling lips and a long, narrow nose. Handsome? Not. Sex on a stick? No way. Yet there was something about him. She couldn't figure out what it was, but it caught her attention, and made her wonder what it would be like to kiss him.

She shuddered inwardly and hoped he couldn't tell. He was the last man on the planet she had any business being attracted to.

Especially when her role model had been her father, who would have been appalled at the thought.

Harlan put a pile of large sketches on her desk. "I've been working on the *Addams Family* sets like you told me to. I need your okay before I start building on Monday."

With someone else, she might have made small talk. With him, she pulled the sketches to her and prepared to dislike them on principle. She picked up the first one and studied it for a minute. It was all she could do not to say "Oh, wow" and wave it in the air.

It was wonderful.

She was stunned.

Well, shit. His work would definitely be earning her seal of approval.

She looked over the rest of the sketches one at a time. The outside of the mansion and the cemetery next to it were perfect. The derelict mansion loomed, rundown and spooky, and the fog-enshrouded tombstones painted on the back of the set added the perfect shiver.

"You'll want to add dry ice fog from sources behind the fence," Harlan said, handing her yet another picture, this one with an iron and stone fence in front of the painted tombstones. "That should give your actors plenty of room for whatever dance numbers are involved."

"I see," she murmured noncommittally. She loved the sketch, but she'd be damned if she let on. Especially to *him*.

She nodded and picked up the next sketch, this one of the inside of the mansion. The walls were the same painted on stones as the outside of the house. Portraits of creepy Addams ancestors adorned the walls, and wide pillars framed the front door at the back of the stage. A sweep of stairs along one side led to a second level. A row of windows in the back looked out to leafless tree limbs and a shadowy full moon shining down on the family cemetery.

"This wall does double duty." He pointed to the wall on the side. "Inside and outside. With the stairs moved into place, the front door and windows can't be seen."

"Clever," she said, more to herself than to him.

She flipped through the rest of the sketches. It killed her to admit it, but his ideas were wonderful. If he could translate the sketches into a set, they would have the perfect shabby, eerie, faded elegance backdrop for the creepy but hilarious family they were bringing to life this winter. She handed the sketches back to him. "They're good," she said grudgingly.

"Thanks," he said softly. His gaze met and held hers. *Damn.* She hadn't imagined the attraction in his eyes a few minutes ago.

He was as attracted to her as she was to him.

This would not do. Not at all.

In fact, it made her mad. A man like him attracted to her.

Her, attracted to a man like him.

Abruptly she shoved the sketches across the desk to him. "The last performance of *Beauty and the Beast* is a week from Sunday. You can start building any time after that."

His eyes widened at her unfriendly tone. Why he seemed surprised, she didn't know. She'd made her feelings perfectly clear more than once.

She might be forced to work with him, but she'd be damned if she'd pretend to like it. And no way in hell she'd allow the sexual attraction matter. Appealing or not, he was still an ex-con, not the kind of person who belonged at the Durango. Especially with all the children in the Academy. He wasn't the kind of man they needed to be exposed to.

"Fine. I'll do that." He gathered up the papers and stood. He was halfway out the door before he turned around and faced her, his expression as cold as hers. "Look, I know you don't like me, and you don't want me here. But the powers that be overrode you and here I am, so the least you could do is be professional. I'm trying to be."

Rachel curled her lip. "Boo-hoo."

He scowled. "I'm good at my job and you know it."

"It doesn't negate your past."

He stepped back into her office and leaned over the desk. "So you think I don't belong here cuz I've been to prison?"

"You got it. They have no business hiring an ex-con. Any ex-con. I don't care what you did or what you were in for. The law is the law and you broke it."

"Wow, I don't know why they bothered with a judge and jury," he gibed. "All they had to do was call you in and boom—it's all taken care of. You have no idea what I did or why. All you care about is the fact that I spent seven years behind bars."

"Exactly." Her eyes narrowed. "Not that it matters, but what did they get you for? Drugs? Robbery? What'd you do to get your ass locked up for seven years?"

He leaned even closer, close enough she could feel his body heat and smell the mint gum in his mouth. "I killed a man," he said coldly. "I went out, bought a gun, and shot him in cold blood. Given the choice, I'd do the same damn thing again in a heartbeat." He turned on his heel and left her office.

She stared after him in horror as his footsteps echoed down the hall and faded from hearing. *A murderer.* Harlan had killed a man in cold blood, had no remorse, and would do it again. Cold chills ran down her back as she locked her office door and made her way to her car.

My God. What was Josh thinking? What was Cameron thinking? For that matter, what was Miguel thinking? They had to be out of their ever-loving minds.

Maybe Josh and Cameron didn't know. Maybe Miguel had covered for his old buddy. Rachel's fingers trembled as she started the car. That was it. Miguel hadn't told them. But she was going to. Monday morning she was going to march into Josh's office and tell him in no uncertain terms who they had hired. She was going to make damn sure Josh knew exactly what he and Cameron had done. Then they would let him go. They would have to. No way could they justify having a murderer on the payroll.

He was the last thing the Durango Street Theatre needed.

CHAPTER TWO

Harlan

The woman was a first-class bitch. A judgmental shrew who went out of her way to be shitty. If he didn't need the job so damn bad, he'd tell her to take her attitude and her job and shove it up her shapely ass.

But he couldn't. He pulled up to the light and eased on the brake. He needed the job too badly. One of the conditions of his parole was he be gainfully employed. His parole officer knew about the job, had been pleased when he landed it, and the last thing he wanted to do was quit and piss off the woman who literally held his fate in her hands.

Besides, Miguel had called in a favor to get him the job. In all fairness, except for having to deal with the bitch, it was a gift from the heavens. He could use his design skill and creativity, as well as his talent with carpentry and paint. It sure beat installing cabinets for Home Depot, not that he could get a job with them with his record. He was better off than most parolees and he knew it.

Speaking of Miguel. He pulled out his phone and reread the text from his old friend.

B party next Friday. Can u come?

Harlan bit his lip. His old friend was married to an uptown woman these days and was a millionaire in his own right. No telling what fancy-assed people would be there. On the other hand, Miguel had gone out of his way to help since Harlan been released from prison, and he wasn't about to risk hurting the man's feelings by not showing up. He texted a thumb's up and hoped no one from Miguel's new life remembered who he was.

The light turned green and Harlan punched the accelerator. The crappy old truck pulled out from the light, wheezing and chugging as it struggled to get up to speed. It was a real piece of shit, but it had been sitting with the title in the glove compartment in the storage shed behind his sister Carrie's house when she moved in, making it payment-free wheels. Still, it irked him.

He'd spent years daydreaming about having something chill to drive when he could get behind the wheel again. Instead, he was in this shitty clunker poking along and hoping it got him back to Carrie's place in one piece.

Such was the life of an ex-con. Crappy wheels and a fold-out bed in his teenage nephew's bedroom. Plus, a daily dose of contempt from a high and mighty bitch who had it in for people who had broken the law.

No second chances with her. No acknowledgement he'd paid his debt to society with seven years in prison and nearly ten years of his life gone. As far as she was concerned, he was barely a person since he broke the law. Never mind why he did it. He was an ex-con, and in her estimation would never be anything else.

A lot of people agreed with her.

But not everyone. Miguel had gone out of his way to help, landing him the job at the theater as well as work on his construction crews when Harlan wasn't working on theater sets.

Miguel's brother-in-law Cameron and his husband Josh had been the soul of graciousness, as had Maggie and Miranda. Only Rachel had been cold and rude. He was stupid to let her get his goat and irritate him. He needed to ignore her, the way he had the other assholes who'd come his way since he got out of prison.

If only she wasn't so damned sexy.

There was the irony. He'd spent almost ten years locked away from females, and had spent a considerable amount of time daydreaming about fucking them again, and the first one to appeal to him since he was sprung was a bitch of the highest order.

But she was a beautiful one. He had to give her that.

Lustrous black hair falling in ringlets past her shoulders. Exotic facial features that bespoke of mixed heritage, with high cheekbones, wide lush lips, and eyes with the slightest uptilt. Her tawny beige complexion was the perfect foil for dark brown eyes framed by long, curling lashes. And her body. God, what a body. Long legs, lush breasts and an ass to die for. Merely thinking about her made his dick hard.

Damn.

He willed his thoughts elsewhere and took the side street that led to Carrie's house. Her car was in the driveway, and Nathan's bicycle was on the front porch. He parked behind Carrie's car and went through the garage to the kitchen entrance, where he found his sister taking a casserole out of the oven. She was still in her scrubs and looked tired and older than her thirty-three years. "Sure smells good, Sis. Like Mom used to make," he told her.

"This is one of her recipes."

Harlan leaned over and sniffed appreciatively. "It is. I remember it from when I was a kid."

Carrie smiled briefly before turning back to the dish. Damn. He wished his sister would smile more often. She was so pretty when she smiled. But maybe she didn't think she had much to smile about. She was struggling to bring up two teenagers on her own with what she could earn working long hours as an LVN in a nursing home. She'd wanted to earn an RN and maybe go even higher, but her dreams had gone by the wayside even before his, and she'd struggled for years working as a CNA just to earn the LVN. He'd long dreamed of helping her when he was released, but at this point she was having to put him up, and it didn't look like he was going to be able to do a damn thing for her any time in the near future.

"Anything I can do to help?" he asked.

"Sure. Peel a couple of cucumbers and douse them with vinegar. I'll get Nathan and Evie to set the table and get us drinks." She put both fingers in her mouth and let out an ear-piercing whistle.

Harlan flinched and turned his head. "Damn. You trying to wake the dead?"

"No, only my kids."

It was only a matter of seconds until twelve-year-old Evie skidded into the kitchen on her stocking feet. "Hi, Uncle Harlan. Whatcha need, Mom?" She grinned impishly at Harlan and her mother.

"Set the table. If Nathan doesn't get here you can get the drinks."

"Okay. But I think Nathan's coming. He was shutting down his computer."

Evie started on the table. Fourteen-year-old Nathan appeared a moment later and without being asked started getting out glasses. They really were nice kids, despite the SOB who'd fathered them. They both favored their small, fair mother in looks and in temperament. He could tell they had reservations about him, no doubt because what he'd done and who he'd done it to, but Evie at least was coming around. Nathan still held him at arm's length, not sure what to do with his uncle who'd invaded their lives and taken up residence in his bedroom.

Together they got dinner on the table. The kids didn't have a great deal to say as they devoured the casserole. Evie ducked out as soon as she'd loaded her plate and her silverware into the dishwasher. Nathan loaded his dishes as well but sat back down at the table. "Mom, Andy asked me if I wanted to go to his house to play Fortnight."

Carrie leveled a look at him. "Is his mother working the night shift?"

Nathan looked at her sullenly. "She always works the night shift. You know that."

"And you know how I feel about teenagers home alone and unsupervised. He can come over here like he always does. You know he's always welcome."

Nathan glanced at Harlan and gave her a you've-got-to-be-kidding look. "Mom. Where are we supposed to go to play? It's okay. Never mind." He got up and left the table.

"At least he was polite about it," she murmured.

"Damn, I'm sorry," Harlan said quietly. "Would it help if I went somewhere for a few hours?"

"You're not going anywhere," Carrie said sharply. She took a deep breath. "Absolutely not," she said more calmly. "This is your home too, at least for now. You are always welcome in this house. Nathan understands."

"It's one thing to be welcome. Another to be a serious inconvenience."

"You're not an inconvenience. And even if you were, you'd still be more than welcome." She swallowed. "Damn it, you saved me. If it weren't for you, I wouldn't be here raising my children. I wouldn't even be alive. So don't sweat it. Got it?"

"Got it."

She leaned over and gave him a peck on the cheek. "I love you, Harlan." She scooped her dishes up and put them in the dishwasher. "Let's get this kitchen cleaned up and then we can see what's on Netflix tonight."

Yeah, he'd saved her, he thought later as he laid on the fold out camp bed parked awkwardly in the middle of Nathan's room. He glanced over at his nephew, snoring softly in the twin bed pushed up against the wall. Harlan had kept his sister safe and made it possible for her to raise her children. Given the same situation, he'd do it again in a heartbeat. He'd done what he had to do and he had no regrets.

But, God. The price he'd paid.

He turned over and stared out the window. Seven years of his life gone. Ten, really, given the time he'd lost before the trial and the subsequent years spent as a guest of the State of Texas. His twenties were history. While his friends were getting their educations and starting their careers, he'd been building crap in the prison carpentry shop, learning a skill he'd never intended to learn, but now was the only way he had to make a living and adhere to the conditions of his parole.

He had about half of a college degree he'd gotten in prison. Core courses he'd need for any BA degree, but he had no idea what college courses to take next, or even what direction he wanted to go. His longtime dream of becoming a baseball coach was off the table since his conviction disqualified him from getting a teaching certificate in Texas.

Other professions were out as well. Texas had some of the most restrictive regulations in the nation when it came to convicted felons getting professional licenses. There were things open to him, of course. But he hadn't investigated the list exhaustively, and he wasn't sure he wanted to do any of them.

He really needed to start crafting a plan for his future. With ten years gone, he was woefully late getting started with the rest of his life. He didn't have the luxury of trying things out or taking too long making up his mind.

And there was the rub. Ten years gone, and a lot of doors shut to him now, and his only skill was doing something he half enjoyed, and it didn't allow him to be his own boss and make the kind of money he wanted to build his future.

It was times like this he envied Miguel for all he'd accomplished. Harlan wouldn't have been rich like Miguel, but he would've been out of college, teaching and coaching baseball, and living his dream if he hadn't done what he did.

Thirty-one years old, living in his sister's house, driving a clunker, working for someone else, and trying to figure out how to pay for another college course or two. To top it all off, he had to deal with a bitch who wouldn't cut him any slack. The sad part was he couldn't see much changing.

He'd get his own place sooner or later and some decent wheels when he could afford them, and hopefully scrape together a little tuition money. But what he really wanted to do was no longer an option and he didn't know what he to replace it with.

It would be years before he could fulfill any kind of dream at all. Hell, he'd be staring forty in the face before he could accomplish much of anything.

But for now, he was working with his hands for whoever was willing to hire a man with a prison record, and putting up with people like Rachel who judged him and dismissed him.

She was right about one thing.

He was fucked.

***

Rachel

Rachel parked her car and unlocked the back door of the theater. It was later than she'd planned to come in, but Granny had a doctor's appointment and Rachel or Amy always went along. Granny had a way of hearing what she wanted to hear and not what the doctor said, so they talked to the doctor themselves, not that they had much control if Granny decided to make a pecan pie and eat half of it, to hell with the "sugars." *Abuela* was equally hard-headed about her diabetes, wolfing down flour tortillas every damn day. Lucky Rachel. Diabetes on both sides of the family. Their mother had been diagnosed five years ago, and if she and her sisters didn't end up stabbing their fingers and avoiding cake for the rest of their life, it'd be a miracle.

She unlocked her office door and threw her purse in the drawer. She started toward Josh's office, but heard voices and decided to wait until he was alone. She was planning to confront him with what she'd learned about Harlan and she didn't want anyone else weighing in. She waited a few minutes, and when she heard his office door open and Miranda call out a cheery 'See you later,' Rachel smiled to herself. Miranda was so happy these days, having kissed and made up with the daughter of her heart and resumed her romantic relationship with the girl's father. Recovering alcoholic Ross Ellis wouldn't be her choice for a boyfriend, but he was a decent, kind man now that he was sober, and if he made Miranda happy, more power to them.

At least Ross wasn't a criminal.

Now for the talk with Josh. Rachel squared her shoulders and marched into his office. "Where ya been?" he asked as he looked up from his computer screen.

"I took Granny to the doctor. Her A1C's up again. She fibs about it so one of us goes with her."

"Ah, yes. Grandmothers. Can't live with them, can't live without them. So what can I do for you?"

"You can listen to me for a few minutes and make an intelligent, informed decision based on the facts."

"I already said I'd like to do *Priscilla* if *Kinky Boots* falls through."

Rachel laughed. "For once I'm not here to campaign for an edgy production." She took a breath. "You need to let Harlan Burke go and find another set designer."

Josh's eyes narrowed. "Why? You didn't like the set ideas he came up with?"

"No, they were great. Wonderful. Which is what makes this so sad. I'm sorry, Josh. But based on what I learned about him on Saturday, there's no way we can or should keep him on here at the theater." She leaned forward. "He's a murderer. He killed a man in cold blood. He said so himself. He said he went out and bought a gun and blew him away, and given the same set of circumstances, he'd do it again. I'm assuming you didn't know when you agreed to hire him, or you would have turned Miguel down. We can't have Harlan working in the theater. I don't care how much we owe Miguel."

Josh looked at her with exasperation. "Are you finished with the tirade?"

"That wasn't a tirade. That was me making my case."

"It was a tirade, and you're sorely mistaken. Cameron and I were aware of Harlan's record when we agreed to hire him. Miguel was forthcoming when he talked with us. We knew exactly what he'd done. *Exactly.* Which you don't, or you wouldn't be in here howling that he has to go."

"What do you mean, I don't know exactly what he's done. I know damn well what he did. He came out and told me. He shot a man. Dead. That's all I need to know."

"No, it isn't. You need to know a hell of a lot more before you start with your usual judgmental crap." He shook his head. "Google the case. It's there. What happened. Then maybe you'll see it wasn't all black and white."

"Josh, you know I'm not much one for shades of gray and I'm not gonna apologize for it. Harlan may be as nice as he can be, probably is, but what he did was wrong. I don't care what the extenuating circumstances were or how personable he might be, he took a man's life. I don't see how it can be all right under any circumstances."

"I didn't say it was all right. I said it wasn't all black and white because it wasn't. A lot of people would've done the same thing, and a lot more would admit they'd be tempted. And at the risk of pissing you off, as a cop your father would've most likely agreed with them."

"A lot more would lock him and the others like him away and throw away the key. Maybe if they'd tried it, Daddy would still be alive and we could ask him how he felt." She leaned across the desk. "Daddy was gunned down in cold blood by an ex-con. On a goddamned traffic stop. Ex-cons are bad news. Even if they don't start out that way, they learn it in prison. Harlan was already violent, and he had years in prison to learn more. I'm sorry if I seem like a hard-ass, but *we don't need him.*"

Josh looked at her impatiently. "Harlan's case isn't anything like what happened to your father. A lot of people would say what he did was justified, and I promise you he's no danger to anyone here at the theater. We *do* need him and we're not firing him because you have a bug up your ass about ex-cons."

"You are gonna fucking regret it sooner or later."

"Do what I said. Google him. Find out what happened before you come marching in here making ridiculous demands."

"Whatever. I can Google him until we have unicorns farting in the lobby and it's not gonna make a bit of difference. We don't need ex-cons working here. Not around a bunch of children. Please think about it."

She stomped out of his office and slammed the door behind her. She didn't know what the hell was with him and Cameron. Hiring a murderer. Hiring an ex-con was bad enough. But a murderer? They were out of their minds?

She slammed her own door as well and sat down at her computer. She started to Google his name, but no. It wouldn't matter what she found. It wouldn't matter what circumstances surrounded the incident.

Harlan was an ex-con. A murderer. He was bad news. He didn't belong at the Durango, and nothing on the face of the earth was going to change her mind about it.

CHAPTER THREE

Rachel

Amy whistled under her breath as Rachel turned into the gated subdivision. "Hells bells, I knew Miguel and Vivi had money, but I had no idea how much. Jesus, this neighborhood must cost a fortune," she breathed.

Rachel got out her phone and pulled up to the keypad. "Think, Amy. If Miguel has the money to buy the Durango and rent it to us for a dollar a year because it makes his wife happy, the man's loaded. Although now that Heiser Steel's back on its feet, she's not exactly poverty stricken either." The massive gates parted and she drove through.

Amy leaned forward and pointed out the window. "Would you get a load of that house? You could get lost in there. Has anybody said anything about them living out here?"

Rachel shrugged. "We're probably the only ones who are impressed. Maggie's sister is married to a Navarro heir and Maggie says Misty's place is half again as large, and Josh's grandmother has a huge old home in Monte Vista. Kevin grew up in an Alamo Heights mansion and even Wade's mother is married to money. We da po folks, big sister. Even Felicia."

They both laughed. The Castillo sisters were anything but poor, and they knew it.

"Good point. So how is it that Miguel and Harlan are friends? They're definitely from two different worlds."

Rachel's lips tightened. "Miguel grew up in the 'hood and wouldn't've come nearly so far if Vivi's dad hadn't taken him under his wing. He and Harlan went to school together. Whatever I might think about having to hire Harlan, Miguel's loyal to the old friends he grew up with."

"Speaks well of Miguel. Vivi doesn't have a problem with it?"

"She doesn't have a snotty bone in her body. Still, I think making us hire Harlan was a bit extreme, I don't care how much we owe Miguel."

"Are your panties still in a twist? Jesus, Rachel, it's been a week. Miguel went to bat for him, Josh and Cameron hired him, and he's not going anywhere. So chill. Besides, there must be a lot more to it than you or me knows. Miguel wouldn't be so loyal if he didn't have good reason."

"I don't understand any of 'em. But you're right. I've said my piece and was ignored. There's nothing more I can do."

The GPS indicated a right turn. "Speaking of ex-cons, Leshawn contacted me again."

"I thought you were going to tell him you weren't interested," Rachel said sharply.

"I did. I told you it wasn't going to do any good and it didn't. He texted me again the next day and said he wanted to see me."

"Well, hell. You turned him down, right?"

"Of course. I also told him I wasn't playing hard to get, and I've moved on and that he needs to do the same. It's a shame I don't have a boyfriend to wave under his nose."

"Do you really want one of those, considering your track record?"

"That's right. Stick it right between the ribs," Amy groused. "But you have a point. It does makes me feel uneasy, though. Knowing he's out there thinking he wants to revive things."

"Well, sure. I'd feel uneasy too." Rachel turned one more corner. "We appear to have reached our destination, and from all the cars so has everyone else in San Antonio."

They parked halfway down the block. The party was in full swing and could be heard all the way down the street. Miguel's brother-in-law Cameron threw open the door before they had a chance to knock. "Come on in. The buffet's in the dining room, and Vivi has booze at the bar and more on the patio. Birthday boy's in the big family room."

They snaked their way through the crowded living room and past the food, hoping to greet Miguel. But the crowd around him was three deep, so they spoke to Vivi before doubling back and loading plates with San Antonio delicacies such as tamales and jalapeno poppers.

The house was packed and noisy, and when Amy headed for the less populated patio Rachel followed her gratefully, where she found Josh chatting with Vivi's mother and a woman who looked like an older version of Miguel. Rachel introduced Amy to Betsy Heiser, who in turn introduced them to Juliana Abonce. Josh commandeered the poolside table and they all sat. Rachel looked through the plate glass windows to the crowded family room. "Looks like everyone and God are here tonight." She took a bite of tamale. "Oh, oh, *oh*. This is the best tamale I've ever put in my mouth. Food orgasm!"

Amy bit into hers and her eyes widened. "Ohmygod, you're right. Delicious."

"Why, ladies, thank you." Miguel's mother beamed.

"Wait a minute. You made these?" Amy demanded.

Juliana nodded and Betsy Heiser patted her stomach. "I've gained ten pounds since Miguel and Vivi married." She jabbed her thumb at Juliana. "And every one of them's her fault."

"Sorry." Juliana's eyes danced while looking anything but contrite. "I'm glad you ladies got here in time to get a few. Between the Durango crowd and all of Miguel's old friends, they'll be gone in a half hour."

Rachel and Amy looked at one another. "Do you ever make them for other people? Our mom's birthday's coming up and they'd be perfect for her party," Amy said.

"All the time." She gave them a reasonable price and whipped out her card. "Call me Monday and I'll put you on the calendar."

Rachel and Amy thanked her profusely. Juliana glanced in the window and broke into a smile. "And, speaking of Miguel's old friends, one of his oldest just got here. I'm so glad he's here. He had to leave us for a while."

"Has he been away long?" Betsy asked.

Juliana's lips tightened. "Too long. He should've never had to go away in the first place."

Rachel blinked and glanced over at the plate glass windows. Sure enough, Harlan was stepping into the family room. He was immediately mobbed by a crowd of men and women about his age, and even Miguel walked across the room to give him a hug. "Welcoming the Prodigal Son," Rachel murmured under her breath. She wondered what the hell Juliana was talking about. Apparently Miguel's mother was willing to give Harlan a complete pass for what he did. Damned if she understood it.

Amy glanced over at her, and Josh shot her a look of warning. Rachel nodded slightly. She wasn't about to say something unkind in front of Miguel and Vivi's mothers. Even if she couldn't fathom why they all seemed so enamored of the man.

She and Amy chatted with the moms and polished off their food. Several *Addams Family* cast members wandered out and Amy excused herself to go speak to them. Rachel excused herself as well and got a tequila sunrise from the patio bartender. Clutching her drink like a lifeline, she made her way into the crowded family room, stopping to chat with the Durango people as she edged around a ton of people heading in Miguel's direction. It was slow going. Between her friends from the theater wanting to talk about *Addams Family* and other theater gossip, and the crowd continuing to mill around Miguel and Harlan. Out of the corner of her eye she watched as Harlan was greeted with smiles, high-fives, handshakes, and hearty bro hugs. She couldn't understand the enthusiasm. It was more than their being glad to see him. It was like Harlan was a hero home from fighting a war, not from sitting in prison for murder.

Her curiosity burned, but she'd bite off her tongue before she would ask about it.

The crowd finally thinned some and she made her way over to Miguel and Harlan. "Happy Birthday, old man," she said as she gave Miguel a hug. "Great party. I love your mom's tamales."

Miguel grinned. "She does know her way around a tamale."

She turned to Harlan and her senses went on full alert. He was looking good tonight in new jeans and a green shirt, which brought out the green in his hazel eyes. His hair had been freshly cut and was styled and not falling in his face. His eyes sparkled and face had lost its usual tense expression, making him look younger than he usually did. Her heart did a little thump and she resisted the urge to reach out and touch his hand.

Damn it. He hadn't lost any of his appeal in the last week. She was still attracted to him, at least her body was, and there didn't seem to be much she could do about it.

It irked her no end.

But this was a party and she would by damn be polite, so she forced herself to smile and hoped the smile appeared genuine. "'Evening, Harlan. Doing okay?"

He nodded. "Miguel's wife throws a lovely party, doesn't she?" His smile was as pasted on as hers was.

Miguel turned to Harlan. "My man here tells me the sets for *Addams Family* are designed and he starts building them on Monday. So tell me. Do you like them?" His eyes darted from her to Harlan and Rachel wondered if Miguel knew how she felt about his childhood friend.

Be damned if she'd let on tonight. "They're very good. Quite wonderful, in fact." She smiled at Miguel as she poured on the charm. "But then, I'd expect nothing less. Josh and Cameron were most impressed with the work at the senior center. Harlan, have you told him what you came up with?"

Harlan's eyes widened. "No, not really." She spared him a glance. What did he think she was going to do, dis his work to

Miguel? She could admit his work was wonderful and still not want him at the theater.

"I'd love to hear about them," Miguel prompted.

Harlan's smile turned genuine, and in a few sentences told Miguel about his designs. She listened quietly, occasionally adding a comment or two. She was surprised at this Harlan. Not only was he appealing to her physically, but the man was nice. Seriously nice, and talented as well. Which made it even a bigger shame about him being *a murderer*.

By the time Harlan was finished Miguel had a huge smile on his face. "I knew you'd be good. I'm glad they took you on. You'll really be an asset over there, won't he, Rachel?"

Harlan looked at her warily and she felt the blood rush to her face. "I, uh, I'm sure," she murmured.

She would've said more but another of Miguel's friends elbowed forward and shook Miguel's hand before clasping Harlan around the shoulders. "Harlan, my man. Damn, it's good to see you again. How ya doin? How are Carrie and the kids? Have you seen Jacob and Angela yet? They're dying to see you."

Rachel excused herself and moved away, leaving the three old friends to play catch-up without her. Another member of the Harlan Burke fan club. She'd be damned if she understood these people. They were absolutely enamored of him.

A part of her was curious to the point she was tempted to slip into the bathroom and Google his name. But she wouldn't do it. It didn't matter, the extenuating circumstances everyone else seemed to think were so important. It didn't matter how nice he was or how fond they all were of him. He killed a man. That was the important thing, and she wouldn't let herself get on the rationalization train.

She sneaked another look in his direction. Yep, he was ringing her bells tonight. All her bells. She shook her head. She didn't want him ringing any of them.

Rachel finished her drink and milled around for another hour or so, her pleasure in the party dimmed somewhat by Harlan's continued presence. She was about to round up Amy so they could thank their hostess and leave when Amy approached her with her phone in her hand and worry on her face. "He sent me another text," she said without preamble. "I think he knows where I am."

"Give me that. I want to see."

Amy handed over the phone. *Hey SP. Lookin good 2nite. Can't hide from L so don't try*

Rachel handed back the phone. "'SP'? L?"

Amy swallowed. "He always called me 'Sugar Pie'. The 'L' would be Leshawn." She looked at Rachel with apprehension. "It sounds like he knows where I am."

"It does. But I don't see how he'd know. There weren't any strange cars on our street when we came over here, and on the off chance he followed us, he couldn't've gotten past the security gate."

"But he said I was looking good," Amy protested. "How would he know if he hadn't seen me?"

"Maybe because it's Saturday night and you always look good on Saturday night. Amy, he lived with you for months and he knows you well. Doesn't mean he literally saw you tonight."

"It's the tone. It's like he's threatening me or something."

"He is. The 'can't hide' business. But I really don't think he's out there tonight. I don't know about you, but I'm ready to thank Vivi and go. You?"

"Yeah, sure. Aw, shit. We're parked halfway down the block."

"We'll be fine." She leaned forward. "I'm packin'."

"So? You'd have to get it out of your purse," she whispered back.

"Would you ladies like me to walk you to your car?"

Rachel jumped at the sound of Harlan's deep voice right behind her. She whirled around to find him standing inches away. "Oh, no, that's all right. We'll be fine."

"Rachel, don't be a twit," Amy said. "If this gentleman's willing to escort us to the car, I'm happy to take him up on it." She turned to Harlan with a big smile. "Hi, I'm Amy, Rachel's sister, and I would be more than delighted to take you up on your offer. Give us a minute to thank our hostess." She shot Rachel a 'so there' look.

Rachel shot her one back. *Traitor.*

***

Harlan

It was all Harlan could do not to laugh out loud.

Rachel so didn't want to take him up on his offer. But she had been overridden. By her own sister, no less. He bet it stung.

But he didn't blame the sister for being concerned. If it was the same Leshawn who'd been three cells down from him, the man was an asshole who was born an asshole and would always be an asshole. He was more than capable of harassing a woman. Or worse. From what he'd overheard, it sounded like Amy was an old love interest. So Harlan would walk the ladies to the car and piss off Rachel in the process.

It was the most fun he'd had all week.

But it was about time he left as well, as nice as the evening had been. He'd dreaded coming and had almost called at the last minute and begged off. But far from the glances and whispers he'd expected, his old friends welcomed him with open arms, glad to see him and in some cases openly admiring him. One old buddy even saying, "Wish I had your balls."

He appreciated the kindness but wasn't sure he deserved it. Justified or not, necessary or not, he had taken Cole Abernathy's life. But far from condemning him, the guys from the 'hood seemed to think he was some kind of vigilante hero. A part of him relished the affirmation, especially after Rachel's undisguised contempt. But the part of him who remembered Cole on the front step in a puddle of his own blood recoiled at the thought of him being a hero.

He'd done what he had to do, but he wasn't a hero by anybody's definition.

He wished Miguel a good evening, thanked the lovely Vivi, and was waiting on the front porch when Rachel and Amy appeared. Amy looked around apprehensively.

"Amy, it's all right," Rachel said a little impatiently. She looked over at Harlan. "Shall we go?"

Harlan nodded and before she could stop him, he placed her arm in his. "My mama says a gentleman always takes the lady's arm," he said when she started to object. "Which way?"

Amy gestured in the opposite direction from his truck. "We're in Rachel's wheels tonight."

They walked down the street together, Rachel stiff beside him and Amy still looking around. "I swear I feel like someone's watching me," she murmured. "My spidey sense must be working overtime."

"It is," Rachel said. "But you have good reason. The SOB's contacted you three times in the last week. You've told him you're not interested, but he's not taking the hint."

If it was the same Leshawn, the asshole wasn't going to take a hint. Harlan started to say something to that effect, but Amy was already spooked and he'd be damned if he said anything to remind Rachel where he'd spent the last seven years. Besides, they already knew he'd been eavesdropping, they didn't need to know he'd heard everything.

"If it's any consolation, I don't see how anyone could have followed you in here. The gate damn near closed on the back of my pickup. Not that it would have been much of a loss," he said.

"Wheels is wheels," Rachel said. "Speaking of, we appear to have reached mine."

They stopped in front of a new Dodge Charger he'd admired more than once. He whistled under his breath. "Sweet."

"Until she has to make the payment," Amy teased. She turned to Harlan. "Thanks again. I really appreciate the escort," she said warmly.

He nodded and looked over at Rachel. "Thanks," she murmured quietly.

"You ladies are most welcome. Rachel, I'll see you at the theater." Without giving her a chance to answer, he turned and half-jogged down the street to his truck.

He unlocked the door, tugging a little when it wouldn't open easily. What he wouldn't give for wheels like hers, he thought as he turned the crank and the engine coughed to life. But he was more interested in the woman herself. She was an enigma. She didn't like him, had no use for him, and wanted him gone. At the same time, she admitted she liked his work and even helped him describe it to Miguel.

She didn't seem cold and unfriendly with anyone else. She was quite charming and pleasant to everyone at the theater and it was obvious they liked her a lot. She didn't seem like an unkind woman in general, so there had to be something more fueling her attitude toward ex-cons. He couldn't imagine what had caused her to be so damned prejudiced against him. And prejudice was what it was. Plain and simple.

But he had every intention of finding out. He drove through the imposing gates and took the thoroughfare leading to the expressway. He'd quit avoiding her at the theater. He'd seek her out and let her get to know him and find out there was more to him than his past and the unfortunate label it saddled him with. It'd be a challenge, but before he went to prison he'd always loved those.

Maybe prison hadn't changed him all that much. Maybe he was still up to the challenge that was Rachel Castillo. She interested him more than any woman he'd met since being on the outside. He was damned well going to break through her wall of prejudice and get to know her better. And let her get to know him.

Even if she fought him all the way.

Chapter Four

Rachel

Rachel gave a whoop and did a fist pump in the air. "We landed it," she screamed as she smothered Josh in a huge hug. "We've really got *Kinky Boots*. I swear I will love you forever." Josh felt they were going out on a limb, but agreed to the production anyway.

"You'd love me forever anyway," Josh said as he picked her up and twirled her around. "But yeah, we're doing *Kinky Boots*. We're the first community theater in South Texas to put it on."

"Wade and Owen are gonna be so excited. Is Cameron willing to do another show? Are you?"

Josh looked at her and started laughing. "Rachel, most of the characters in the play are straight, and all of us can play either way. Brian would be wonderful as Charlie."

"He would. Kevin would be good in one of those roles, too. I wonder who'd be the best Lola? Wow. I haven't been this excited about an upcoming production in a long time, and I always get excited."

"I hear you. I'm excited too." He picked her up and whirled her around again.

"So when do we do it?"

"It's not scheduled yet. But within the year, for sure."

"I can hardly wait."

"Me, too. We'll all get together one night on my patio to celebrate. Steaks for the grownups and burgers for the little kids."

"Sure getting to be a lot of those," Rachel laughed. "Julie Abonce, Everly Summerset, Jessica and Brian's two, your two. Regular population explosion."

"Doncha love it?" Josh grinned. "I'll talk to Cam and we'll set up something." He did a soft-shoe all the way down the hall to his office.

Rachel went to her office and was reading the manuscript of *Jesus Christ Superstar* and wondering if it would go over in heavily Catholic San Antonio when the noise began. It wasn't too loud at first, mostly the sound of objects being moved around. But then the god-awful roar of a chainsaw started up. Telling herself the irritating sound was necessary, she closed her door to shut some of it out and took care of the rest with headphones playing the soundtrack of *Kinky Boots.*

She finished reading *Jesus Christ Superstar,* read through *Godspell* and was looking at *Finian's Rainbow* when Josh stuck his head in the door, his eyes snapping with enthusiasm, and said something she couldn't understand. "Give me a minute." She yanked off her headphones and made a face at the sound of a nail gun. "Sorry. I had to blank out the noise somehow. Whatcha need?" she said, raising her voice over the racket.

"I took a look at the first piece of the *Addams Family* set. It is incredible. Awesome. You're gonna love it."

"I'm sure I am," she said dismissively. She had no doubt it was good, based on what she knew of Harlan's work. But she had no desire to see it this morning. She had no desire to be around him today at all. She was still irked with herself. She had no business being attracted to him. She certainly had no business liking him. She needed to stay as far away from him as possible.

But Josh wasn't having any of it. "No, I'm serious. You need to get up out of your chair and go look at what he's doing. You'll understand why Cam and I were glad Miguel sent him our way."

"I'll go on my way out the door to lunch," she promised. "By the way, how would you feel about doing *Jesus Christ Superstar?*"

"It wouldn't be any more likely to offend than some of the rest of what we've done. We can look into it."

"*Finian's Rainbow?*"

Josh looked at her disbelievingly. "You want to do blackface in this day and age?"

"We could double-cast the senator," she suggested as the chain saw started back up.

"We could. Let's think about it." Josh disappeared. She donned the headphones and finished reading through the *Finian's Rainbow* and was about to start *Singin' in the Rain* when her stomach growled and she spotted the time on her computer screen. Yowza. It was almost two. She'd worked through lunch hour and breakfast had been skimpy. It was time to go find food somewhere. But first she would go by the stage and see what Harlan had done so far. She had to go by the stage to get to the parking lot anyway, unless she walked down the street to the Fruteria.

She made her way through the rabbit warren into the auditorium. A sawhorse sat on one side of the stage. A tall set piece stretched across the other side, with a huge paint tarp down along its length and four open paint cans sitting to one side. Harlan had his back to the chairs and was on a tall ladder. The set piece in front of him was already painted the gray-beige of an old stone wall and he was drawing in the individual stones, shading them to look like real stone. She watched him work for a couple of minutes, making the set piece which would double as the inside and outside wall of the Addams mansion came to life. She could see where he'd already sketched in the window and door that would be visible "outside" but not when the inside set was in use. To one side was a stack of "portraits" of various Addams Family members. The top one, the one of Morticia, looked almost exactly as Amy would be in her Morticia makeup and wig. Rachel stared for a moment, dumfounded, wondering how he had known.

Amy hadn't even tried on her wig yet.

Harlan drew in a couple more stones and then backed down the ladder. He turned around and his eyes widened when he spotted her standing in the orchestra pit. "Did I disturb you?" he asked as he smiled at her.

"No, you disturbed me about four hours ago."

He grinned unrepentantly. "Sorry about that." He turned from the ladder.

"No harm done. Headphones and a closed door do wonders." She gestured with her arm. "Lookin' good."

"Why don't you come up and take a closer look?"

"Don't mind if I do."

She ran up the side steps and onto the stage. Up close, the "stone wall" looked even better. He'd shaded in the stones so they were variegated as real weathered stones would be. "Sweet," she breathed as she reached toward the wall, careful not to touch the wet paint. "How are you getting this effect?"

"Let me show you." He picked up the narrow brush and dipped it in the black paint. In a few strokes he drew in a stone. Then he used the other paint colors to shade it in. There was no way she could contain her enthusiasm. "Harlan, what you've done so far looks wonderful. Absolutely wonderful. I love it."

"Thanks." He looked proud and embarrassed at the same time.

She wandered over to the stack of the family portraits. "May I?" She gestured to the stack.

"Sure. They're dry."

She picked up Morticia's painting off the top. "This looks exactly like Amy will look in costume. How did you know?"

"I went online and looked at the characters from the old movies and other stage productions. Your costumes won't be so different."

"But you got Amy's face."

"I did Morticia Sunday after meeting Amy at the party. I also did Grandma Addams. She was at the party too." He handed her a second portrait. "Did I nail this one as well?"

Rachel took one look at Letti as Grandma Addams and burst out laughing. "You did. But we're not showing this to her yet. Not until she sees herself made up as Grandma for the first time. She's already sensitive about getting older."

"The way the stud muffin she's married to looks at her, she's got no cause to worry." She wasn't sure but she thought she caught a touch of wistfulness in his tone.

"No, she doesn't. What about the rest of the portraits?"

He grinned. "That's where I need a little help. Do you have headshots of the rest of the cast? I've sketched in everything but their faces." He showed her Gomez's picture, sketched and partially painted but with the face missing.

"Sure. Or you can come by rehearsal a couple of nights from now and meet them all in person."

"Won't I be disturbing your rehearsal?"

"We can spare a couple of minutes."

"Thanks. It would help. And thanks for the kind words. I love how it's coming together." His eyes shone and his smile was wide.

Rachel nearly gasped. It was the first time she'd seen him really smile since he'd come to the Durango. It lit up the room and warmed her from her head to her toes.

Damn. She was responding to him again.

It was the last thing she wanted to do, but it was damned hard not to. He was physically appealing, he was nice, and today he was charming as well. And his enthusiasm was contagious.

The combination was overwhelming.

"Okay, then. I'll look for you Thursday night," she said briskly. "We start at seven. See you there."

Harlan nodded. His smile faded. "Is Amy okay?"

"You mean has the asshole contacted her again. No, he hasn't. Thank God. I hope he took the hint."

"Tell her not to let her guard down," he said seriously. "He...guys like him never give up easily."

Rachel wondered at Harlan's tone. It was like he knew something she didn't. She brushed aside the thought. "Gotta go. Again, I love what you've done already. It's gonna be awesome."

Harlan smiled again. "Thanks. I think so too. Are you off for a coffee break?"

"No. I got busy and forgot to eat lunch. I need to get some food in me or I'm gonna face plant on my desk."

"I missed lunch, too. Why don't we go down the block and grab something at the fruit place?"

Her smile faded. "Harlan, I don't think so." She waited for his smile to disappear and his wariness to return.

But to her surprise his smile remained. "I do think so. We'd have a nice lunch together."

It was on the tip of her tongue to agree. *Remember who he is,* she admonished herself. *Remember who he is and what he's done.* "Honestly, I'll pass. But thanks."

"Hmm. I bet I can read your mind about now. You don't want to go get a cup of fruit with the local ex-con. The dubious guy with the shady past and the shitty label. The label you can't seem to get past, even though I know you're really a nice woman. How'm I doing?"

Rachel felt her face flame. "Pretty damned well." She looked him in the eye. "I admit to all of it. But I have reasons for feeling the way I do. Good reasons."

"Reasons you can't put aside long enough to eat a cup of fruit with me? I'm sure you can put your doubts aside for one short hour and see me as another human being, see me as a man and not a label. Who knows, you might be able to see me without it after the hour is up. Why don't we try?"

Rachel thought about it. Could she quit thinking of him as an ex-con and see him as Harlan? For the next hour, she could and she would. After that, probably not.

But she could let herself enjoy his company for the next hour.

"Okay. A cup of fruit it is."

They left the theater and walked side by side down the sidewalk. This close, she could feel the warmth of his body next to hers. He smelled of aftershave and the sawdust lingering on his arms and clothes, an altogether pleasant combination.

The afternoon was hot and the sun shone down brightly. She glanced over at him. It hadn't been obvious in the theater, but in the sun she could see a faint sunburn across his nose and cheeks and a smattering of freckles that hadn't been there a month ago.

He was losing his prison pallor.

She started to comment on the sunburn but thought better of it. Instead, she commented on the new burger joint that had recently opened about a mile down the street. "The folks at the Durango have done their best to keep them in business. Wade and Owen are regulars."

"Who are Wade and Owen?"

"I guess you've never met them. Owen is Letti's ex and the father of her two older children. Wade's his husband."

"What? Her ex is married to a man?" He rubbed his forehead. "Sometimes I forget how much things changed in the years I was locked up. Counting time before the trial, it was almost ten years."

"I never thought about it," she said quietly. Ten years. He had lost a lot of his life.

On the other hand, his victim lost all of theirs.

It didn't seem like a fair trade.

There was a line out the door of the Fruteria. "Oops, I guess this was a mistake," Harlan murmured.

"No worries. The line here moves fast and most of these orders are to-go. We'll have our orders placed and a table before you know it."

They did. Rachel placed her order first and snagged a table right in front of the window. Harlan joined her a moment later with the plastic placard with their order number. "You come here often?" he asked and she almost laughed. She knew he didn't mean it as a pick-up line, but it was tried and true nonetheless.

"Me and everybody else at the theater. We're doing our best to keep these folks in business too."

They sipped their sodas and made small talk until their order arrived. Harlan's banana split towered over the bowl and Rachel's gazpacho filled a big paper cup. She looked at his banana split enviously. "God, I wish," she said as he took a huge bite.

"So why didn't you get one? You certainly don't need to be dieting." He downed another big bite.

She swallowed a spoonful of the cold, spicy soup. "It's not a diet. It's diabetes. I don't have it yet," she hastened to add when his eyes widened. "But both sides of my family are shot through with it. Granny and *Abuela* have had it for years, and Mom was diagnosed five years ago. My sisters and I are already cutting the sugar. Though I did have a piece of Miguel's birthday cake."

"Granny and *Abuela*?"

"Granny Washington and *Abuela* Castillo. Pretty well tells the story of my heritage."

"In one sentence, no less. Interesting."

"It was interesting, all right. Lorene Washington and Raymond Castillo, the Romeo and Juliet of the swinging seventies. Mom and Daddy met in high school and after several years of drama, defied both families and got married. Neither side was wild about them marrying outside their 'community.'" She made air quotes.

"Happy marriage?"

"Very much so, until Daddy died."

"I'm sorry for your loss. It's hard, in this day and age, to imagine that kind of racial prejudice."

"It wasn't all race." Rachel snickered wickedly. "*Abuela* is a staunch Catholic. She dragged *Abuelo* to Mass every time the parish door opened and expected her only son to marry a good Catholic girl in the church. They were appalled when they found out Mom was Baptist and that Granny Washington never married my grandfather, even though their relationship lasted until he died."

"Why didn't they get married?"

"He was a rich white boy. It was illegal in 1955, not that his family would've stood for it anyway. By the time Virginia versus Loving rolled around, he'd married a white girl his parents foisted off on him and had two kids with her. But to his credit, he took good care of Granny and Mom and sent Mom to college." She held out her arm. "Everybody thinks I'm this color because I'm black. It's more the Native American. *Abuelo* was almost full-blooded Coahuiltecan."

"Wherever you got it, you're beautiful." His cheeks turned a little red, but he held her gaze.

"Thanks." She forced herself not to look away.

"Did the families ever come around?"

"It took ten years and three granddaughters, but yeah. Although Granny and *Abuela* are huge rivals, constantly trying to outdo one another. Whose cake is tastier, whose house looks better for Christmas, who can cook the best Thanksgiving turkey, who can come up with the best birthday presents. Sometimes it gets old, but my sisters and I sure get a lot of good food out of it."

"Sisters? You have more than one sister?"

She nodded. "You've met Amy. She's the oldest. I'm the youngest and Felicia's in the middle. Supposedly she lives with Amy and me, but she's got a really high-level government job doing something she never discusses and she's out of town eighty percent of the time. Wouldn't be my cup of tea, but she loves the life. Plus, she's willing to pay a third of the rent for a lovely house close to Fort Sam even though she's almost never there." She grinned. "We call her Pocahontas. She calls me Tiana and Amy Moana."

"Three princesses. Why am I surprised?"

"I have no idea." She winked and swallowed another spoonful of soup. "So I have a question for you. How did you know Miguel? He grew up in the barrio."

"So did I. My stepdad was Hispanic and owned a house on the West Side. My sister and I were practically the only Anglo kids in our school."

His smile faded and Rachel wondered if the crime he committed had anything to do with the neighborhood. "Were you picked on?"

"Once in a while. For the most part they treated the *güero* boy okay and I made a lot of friends. They're loyal, that bunch. When shit hits the fan, they stick."

She nodded. She'd gathered as much Saturday night.

"Are your mom and stepdad still living in the barrio?"

His expression hardened and he shook his head. "They needed money and had to sell the house. We lost Mom a few years ago to cancer and Joe went back to Mexico. His Social Security goes farther down there." His face closed off and Rachel didn't ask him anything more.

They finished their food and got refills on the sodas. He held the door and escorted her out, his hand on her waist as they started back to the theater. The sun was even hotter than it had been on the way over. Or it may have been the heat coursing through Rachel's body as they walked together. His hand was warm on her waist and she was loath to move away, even though she probably should. She'd enjoyed talking with him more than she'd thought she would. The more she was around him, the better she liked him.

Then there was the awareness. They'd interacted as friends, but there had been an underlying current running between them. He'd told her she was beautiful, and he meant it. She had been complimented all her life on her beauty and normally took it in stride, but coming from him it was different somehow. It meant more. It meant a man who interested her, who appealed to her, who she wanted to reach out and touch, felt the same way about her.

This wasn't good, not one damned bit. But right now, she didn't give a damn. She'd worry about it later.

The theater was deserted when they got back, contributing to the feeling of intimacy already enveloping them. "Let's see what it's looking like from the back of the theater," he said, gesturing to the auditorium doors. They ventured into the cavernous darkness. Rachel stepped to the light and sound board and switched on the stage lights, leaving the seating space unlit. Harlan sucked in a breath. "It looks good from back here, too." He reached out and grasped Rachel's hand.

"You knew it would," she said breathlessly. This close, she was conscious of the heat he radiated and the strength of his hand holding hers.

He turned to her and reached out for her with his other hand. "Stop me if you don't want this. Otherwise, I can't go one more minute without kissing you."

She wasn't about to stop him. Throwing all reason to the wind, she melted into his embrace. As close as they were in height, their lips met easily in a kiss that was gentle at first as she savored the touch of his lips on hers and the warmth of his arms around her.

But as their desire deepened, the kiss grew more intimate. His tongue snaked out and sought entrance, which she willingly granted, and then their tongues engaged in an erotic duel. They moved closer, her breasts crushed against his hard muscular chest, her nipples swelling and poking through her clothes. She could feel his cock swell against her, turgid against the vee between her legs. Her heart pounded and her head spun. She'd been kissed before and had enjoyed her share of lovers. But never had a kiss moved her this way. Never had she responded this fast to a man's embrace. This was something special. Different. Out of the ordinary.

At least it was for her. Maybe it was always this way for him.

Right now, she didn't care. She wanted to go on kissing him and touching him. She let her fingers roam over the shirt-covered muscles in his back and shoulders. Her hands drifted lower, cupping his hard ass. His fingers were busy as well, dancing down her back and waist to the gentle curve of her butt. Her head spun. If it felt this good standing up with their clothes on, it would really be something else naked and horizontal.

They kissed for long moments. And would've gone on kissing but for the buzz of Rachel's phone in her pocket. Reluctantly she raised her head. "Ignore it," he said roughly.

"Let me see who it is." She fished her phone out of her pocket. Amy could wait. She started to put away the phone and return Harlan's embrace when a text appeared.

Emergency. Call now.

"Crap. I guess I better take this." Reluctantly, she backed away from Harlan's embrace and punched in Amy's number. "What?" she said crossly.

"He was here, Rachel. At the house." Amy's voice rose in panic.

"Who? Leshawn?" she asked sharply.

"Yeah, Leshawn. He was *here.* At the house. He left a note on my car."

Rachel took a deep breath. "Are you all right? Is he still there?"

"No, I'm not all right. I'm scared shitless."

"Amy. Answer me. Is he still there?"

"I don't know. I don't think so."

"Okay, honey. Calm down. I'll be there in a few minutes. Are you alone?"

"Uh-huh, I'm alone. I hope."

Amy clicked off and Rachel put her phone in her pocket. "I gotta go." She turned and ran back to her office, leaving Harlan standing in the darkened auditorium.

She grabbed her purse and keys and sprinted toward the parking lot like the hounds of hell were chasing her. And not entirely because of Amy. She had to get away. From the theater. From Harlan. From her own weakness. From the desire that threatened to envelop her and rob her of all common sense.

From the danger the impossibly sexy ex-con represented to her.

Chapter Five

Rachel

Rachel clicked open the car door and slid behind the wheel, rubbing her fingers across her still-tingling lips. Her hands shook as she darted and dodged through afternoon traffic cursing the school zones and the clogged thoroughfares. She was a fool for being attracted to Harlan. He was an ex-con. A murderer. A man much like him was frightening her sister. A man much like him murdered her father. Though charming, he was bad news all around and she needed to stay as far away from him as she could.

Her father would be so disappointed.

There would be no more lunches at the Fruteria. There would be no more kissing. He was a colleague she had to work with despite her feelings.

He could never be anything more.

She breathed a sigh of relief when she turned onto her block. She slowed down more than necessary and cruised slowly to her house looking for any cars seemingly out of place. But the vehicles along the street and in the driveways were the same as they always were. She pulled up behind Amy's snappy red crossover and sprinted to the front door. Amy was curled up on the sofa with her head on her knees. She was still dressed in the business slacks and blouse she wore for work, but had kicked off her dress pumps. Rachel took one look at her and made a beeline for the refrigerator. She poured Amy a big glass of ever-present Moscato and handed it over.

Amy swallowed half the glass in a single gulp. "Thanks." She set the wine glass on the coffee table. "You need one too?"

"Come to think of it, I do."

She poured herself a glass and sat down across from Amy. "Do you still have the note?"

Amy gestured to a scrap of paper on the coffee table. Rachel started to pick it up but thought better of it and got two pairs of plastic gloves from the kitchen. They each donned a pair and Rachel picked up the note. "We belong together, Sugar Pie. I'll be around to see you soon."

"Well, hell. Did you see him leave the note?"

"No, I'd just gotten home."

"So exactly, what happened?"

"Mr. Alfonso's wife called and said the baby was sick and he was taking her to the doctor. Since there wasn't much for me to do this afternoon, he told me to take off and I could make up the hours later. I'd parked and had gone in, and out of the corner of my eye I saw someone messing around my car. I started out the door but Leshawn jumped in a late model Lexus and took off. I found the note under the windshield wiper." She took a breath. "Maybe I'm being silly but he scared me. Besides, he knows where I live."

"How did he know where you live? You weren't living here when he was living with you."

"I don't know. Maybe... Oh shit. Maybe he's following me." She turned, her expression pained and frightened. "What do I do?"

"We call the police, that's what. He's an ex-con and he came around even though you told him not to. That warrants a call to the cops."

She punched in 911 and a fresh-faced young patrolman showed up twenty minutes later. He listened to Amy's story and took down some notes. "Let me see if I got this down correctly. He's texted you three times, once a little over a week ago and twice on Saturday." He briefly summarized the contents of the texts and Amy nodded. "Then he came by this afternoon and left a note on your car. Correct?"

"Yes."

"But he didn't approach you or speak to you?"

"No. He took off when I came out the door."

"That's it?"

"I... I guess so. When I looked out the window his Lexus was gone."

"Lexus? I thought you said he was an ex-con." The cop's eyes narrowed suspiciously.

"Drug money," Amy and Rachel said in unison.

"The car's in his grandmother's name," Amy added.

"So he never actually approached you. He left you a note and took off." The policeman looked at Amy.

"But...but...he found me and he came to my house, and he'd never been here before," Amy sputtered. "He left a note after I told him I wasn't interested. He scared the shit out of me. He's an ex-con. Isn't there something you can do?"

"Ma'am, if I arrested everyone in this town who's left behind an unwelcome note, there wouldn't be anyone left on the street. I think you're making a mountain out of a mole hill."

Rachel's jaw dropped. "No, she isn't. She told him she's not interested, and he came over here anyway."

"So tell him again." The policeman looked bored.

"Tell me, officer. What can you do?" Amy demanded. "An ex-con's coming around when I don't want him to and pestering me. What about stalking? I think he's stalking me."

"Ma'am, that would be hard to prove, given a few texts and a note on your car. Has he confronted you face to face? Has he actually spoken to you?"

"Fine," Rachel snapped, her patience gone. "You don't think she's being stalked. I do, but that's beside the point. What can you do?" She nailed the policeman with a glare.

His eyes widened. "I-I guess I can pay him a visit and tell him your sister wants to be left alone."

"You do that. Pay him a visit, lean on him a little. Explain how Amy's not interested any more, and how we have stalking laws in place if he chooses to keep pestering her."

"I'll do that. But honestly, ladies, knowing Leshawn Hayes, do you really think me having a talk with him going to help?"

"No. Yes. Maybe. I don't know," Amy admitted. "Probably not."

"Go ahead and talk to him," Rachel said. "You never know. It might put the fear of God in him."

The policeman choked back a laugh. "Ma'am, if he was as successful a drug dealer to afford a Lexus put it in his grandmother's name, get out of jail and flaunt it, he's not scared of me. But I'll try."

"Thank you," Rachel said.

"Yes, thanks," Amy echoed.

They saw the young cop to the door. "That was a colossal waste of time," Amy murmured under her breath after they shut the door behind him. "You know as well as I do Leshawn's not gonna care what the cop says. Besides, that cop could've cared less and Leshawn's gonna see that."

"Yeah. Pisses me off big-time. You'd think a cop would've been more on our side. Found a way to support us. I like to think Daddy would have."

"Daddy would've given a damn. But then, Daddy had black daughters. Barney Fife there probably barely knows any women of color."

Rachel made a face. "How could he not know women of color? This is San Antonio, for crying out loud. It kind of hurts, you know. Daddy gave his life protecting the people of this town, and now that the shoe is on the other foot, that pissant cop could care less."

"I doubt he knew Daddy. Even if he did, the department has a notoriously short memory when it comes to the families of fallen officers. They were good at first, but then..." Amy made a moue with her lips.

"Yeah, I know."

Rachel changed out of her work clothes into her favorite athletic shorts. Her hands were still shaking, either from the policeman's visit or Harlan's kiss, she wasn't sure which. *Chill.* She needed to chill. She downed the rest of the wine and rummaged around in her purse until she found her earbuds. She went into the sunroom and put on her favorite meditation music, the haunting notes of a Native flute, but switched it off five minutes later finding herself more irritated than relaxed. The normally calming Enya had the same effect, as did the slack key guitar music she'd fallen in love with on a vacation on Maui.

She finally gave up on soothing and put on the soundtrack to the remake of *Footloose,* dancing with Blake in the almost-empty sunroom behind the kitchen. The late afternoon sun poured in, overpowering the already inadequate window A/C unit and bathing Rachel in a golden glow. She danced the entire soundtrack, unconcerned about technique, caring only for the way the ball of stress inside her began to loosen. But relief was slow to come. She danced her way through the entire *Footloose* soundtrack and was halfway through *Anything Goes* before the tight knot in her stomach dissipated to the point she could think about the day without wanting to throw up.

She flopped down on one of the two lounge chairs and picked up the framed photo sitting on the small table between them. A bigger one sat on the bookshelf in the living room, but this was her copy and it always had a place of honor in whatever room she hung out in most. She looked down and touched the picture with her index finger. It was the last picture ever taken of her father a matter of weeks before his murder. They'd gone to the coast for the weekend, and Lorene had snapped the picture as he and his three daughters were coming out of the water together. They were smiling and he had his arm around Rachel and was holding Felicia's hand. He'd been only forty-two, still fit, handsome, and young looking. He'd be forever young, she thought sadly as she stared down at the picture. He'd never grow old or see his grandchildren, if there ever were any.

A violent ex-con had robbed him of the privilege.

An ex-con like Harlan.

Rachel stared out the window at the live oak trees gracing the back yard. She'd shown poor judgment today. She couldn't help her attraction to Harlan. Against her will she found him appealing, and kissing him had been the stuff of dreams. But she could and would handle things with him differently from now on. Charming and sexy as he might be, but he was still a criminal. As Ray Castillo's daughter, she should've already known that. If she didn't know it before, the crap with Leshawn was yet more evidence of what happens when dealing with an ex-con. Harlan wasn't a man she had any business falling for. She needed to stay a mile away from him.

Even if he'd given her the best kiss of her entire life.

CHAPTER SIX

Harlan

Harlan whistled under his breath as he put the finishing touches on the first side wall of the *Addams Family* set. The back wall was built and stood in place waiting to be painted. It'd be painted on both sides and was lightweight enough to be turned around during scene changes. He'd already built the iron fence surrounding the cemetery which would be moved in front of the tombstones, with strategically placed buckets of dry ice to add an eerie fog to the scenes. He had a couple more days of painting before he built the stairs leading to the upper level of the indoor mansion. He capped the paint can and took the paint brushes out to the alley for a quick cleaning before he started sketching.

He could hardly wait to show Rachel what he'd done.

He returned to the stage and with a carpenter's pencil began working on the tombstones. They'd give him the perfect excuse to seek her out. He could ask if she wanted names on them, something he'd usually decide on his own. But he would let her make the decision, and get in a little more flirting with the woman who'd been on his mind night and day since he they'd had a phenomenal kiss. She'd consumed his daytime thoughts and appeared in his dreams at night, naked and alluring as he pounded into her warm, willing body.

But he hadn't seen much of her these past couple of days and wondered what was up as he headed to the offices. In fact, other than from a distance, he hadn't seen her at all. If she was avoiding him, he couldn't figure out why. It didn't seem likely, not after they'd connected so well. They'd talked and laughed as friends, and he'd been amazed she had been so forthcoming about her family's colorful past. Then, he couldn't believe she'd said yes, but damn if he wasn't thrilled she did. They shared a scorching kiss like he'd never shared with a woman in his life. Not that he had a lot to go on. In the years he was imprisoned, he'd missed out on most of the experience men had by the time they were his age. But he still was certain what he and Rachel had shared the other day was far from the norm.

He grinned to himself. Only one way to find out. They'd need to share it again, and plenty more if he had his way.

He stuck his head in her office door. Her back was to the door and she was on the phone. "*Abuela*, an A1C of seven point five is not good, I don't care what Tia Rosa said. Just because yours is lower than hers is doesn't make it good." She was quiet for a minute. "Dr. Hernandez wouldn't tell you any such thing. It might be better than it was, but no doctor in his right mind's going to be pleased with seven point five. Do we have to start going to the doctor with you like we do Granny?" She listened for a minute before holding up her free hand and crossing her fingers. "Below seven. Well below seven. If she can do it, so can you." She listened again and laughed. "Love you too. Bye."

She threw her phone on the desk and whirled around, her smile fading when she saw him at the door. "Harlan. I didn't know you were there."

"No worries. You had a fire to put out." He gestured to the phone. "Did it work?"

Her smile faded entirely. "Did what work?"

"Throwing your Granny up to your *Abuela*. Did it spark her competitive spirit?"

"I don't know. I hope so." She looked at him levelly. "What can I do for you?"

"Two things. First off, I'm getting ready to paint the back set. The one with the gravestones. You want visible names on them, or leave them vague?"

"Names work," she said dismissively. "And second?"

"I have the first piece of the set completely done. You want to see it?"

"I'm sure it's fine. It was looking good the other day."

"Aw, come on," he wheedled. "Come see for yourself."

"All right." She got up out of her chair with all the enthusiasm of a visit to the dentist.

What the hell? His spirit began to take a nosedive. Apparently she'd had second thoughts about kissing the local ex-con.

Well, too damn bad he thought as they walked together to the stage. She kept a more space than was necessary between them. She'd let down her guard the other day and it'd been wonderful. They'd be idiots not to try to see where their awesome connection might take them.

His mom hadn't raised any idiots. He'd bet hers hadn't either.

He'd have to persuade her to see things his way.

The stage lights were on. They entered behind the wall and he motioned her to the front of the stage. She took one look at the finished wall and her eyes lit up. "It's wonderful. Really wonderful. Thank you." For a moment her smile was luminous, but she quickly sobered. "This piece is next?" She gestured to the back wall.

"Yeah. The back side will be painted to match this wall and I'll include a couple of windows looking out on the cemetery. This side will be painted with the tombstones and a dark forest behind them and a spooky looking moon with tree branches, and maybe a bat in front of it. Mostly the shadows of trees in the dark. Unless you want it daylight."

"No. All the outdoor stuff's set at night. Shadows of trees and a spooky looking moon will be great."

"The gates to the mansion will be over here." He gestured to the left side of the stage. "They can stay in place for the most part and won't have to be moved."

"Works for me." She turned to go. "I already have the fence done," he said quickly. "Want to see it?"

"Sure."

He darted backstage for the fence pieces. Damn it, she wasn't brushing him off again. She was going to stay and at least talk to him this afternoon, and accept a date for this weekend if he could persuade her. "This is where the fence'll be," he said, placing a couple of the sections in place. "The base is wide enough to conceal the dry ice buckets. Three of them should be enough."

She nodded. "It will. If that's all…"

"Unless you'd like to take a break for lunch," he said. "We could go back to the fruit place or down to the hamburger place you mentioned the other day." He looked her in the eye and let his interest show. "Pick up where we left off, maybe."

There. He'd made his intentions clear.

She shook her head. "Harlan, I don't think so. But thanks."

He gave her his most charming smile. "What if I said I do think so?" He took a step closer. "The other day was one of the nicest afternoons I ever had, and I said I'd like a repeat."

She took a step back "I really don't think so. I'm flattered, honestly I am. But you and I... We're not such a good match. Trust me."

"Why not?" He pinned her with his gaze. "You enjoyed yourself the other day as much as I did." He lowered his voice. "And our kiss. Damn, that wasn't a usual kiss and you know it as well as I do."

"The kiss was a mistake," she said. "In fact, the whole thing was a mistake on my part. A mistake we won't be repeating."

Harlan's temper flared and he tamped it down. "It wasn't a mistake from my point of view, and at the time it wasn't from yours either. Until you got to thinking about it. What happened? Did you forget I'm a human being and go back to defining me by labels?"

"As a matter of fact, I did," she said regretfully. "Yes, you're a human being and admittedly a charming one. But you're also an ex-con and a murderer. Those are more than labels. It's who you are. I can't get past that."

"They are not who I am," he told her, holding back the snarl he felt creeping on his lip. "Far from it. I'm a helluva lot more than something you know nothing about. I thought we'd gotten past that, but you're clinging to your prejudices."

She looked at him unbelievingly. "Prejudices? I don't want to get involved with a damned murderer and you call me prejudiced? Where the hell do you get off?"

"I call 'em like I see 'em. And I see a narrow-minded woman who won't look past the superficial to what's underneath."

"I know what's underneath," she said levelly. "A criminal. A criminal they shouldn't have hired in the first place. There's no getting around it, as charming as you are and as much as I might like you." She took another step toward him. "I have good reason for the way I feel. A criminal murdered my father. An ex-con who'd just gotten out of prison. Daddy stopped him for a burned-out taillight and he shot my father and killed him in cold blood. You're a murderer. You stood in my office and said so."

"I am not a murderer like he was," Harlan said between clenched teeth. "What I did was nothing like shooting an innocent cop. If you gave enough of a damn to learn the truth, you would've looked up my case on the Internet."

"But that's just it," she snapped. "It doesn't really matter what I might find on the Internet. A murderer is a murderer." She took a breath. "And if losing Daddy to a piece of shit ex-con wasn't enough, another fucking criminal's stalking my sister. Leshawn—"

"Don't you dare put me in the same sentence as an asshole like Leshawn Hayes," Harlan shot back. "I am nothing like that sleaze ball. We don't get to be mentioned in the same damn breath."

"Why not? He's a criminal, you're a criminal. No, you're worse. They got him for dealing drugs. You took a man's life."

"A man who needed to die. Not that you give a damn about that. Oh, no. I killed a man, therefore I'm the lowest of the low, no matter what the circumstances. No matter why I did it. So yeah, you're prejudiced. Prejudiced and narrowminded and judgmental. And a big fucking disappointment. We could've had something nice. But you'd rather cling to your black and white ideas about right and wrong. It's pitiful. Downright pitiful."

"I'm a right and wrong kind of person. And what you did was wrong, I don't care why you did it."

"Hell, you don't even *know* why I did it. So I guess we can add ignorant to your list of stupids."

Her head snapped back so fast her chin went into her neck. Somehow, what he'd said had gotten through. But he'd had enough. She wasn't worth it.

She folded her arms in front of her. "Okay. Enlighten me. What possible excuse can you give me for killing a man?"

"I had to... You know what? I don't have to justify myself to a narrowminded jerk like you. If you give even a little bit of a damn, look it up on the Internet. Otherwise, you stay out of my way and I'll stay out of yours."

His entire body vibrated as he stormed off the stage and out to the parking lot. He was furious with himself. He'd been stupid in the extreme to think he'd broken past her objections, no matter how scorching their kiss. She'd gone back to that shit about him not belonging at the Durango even though she was wild about the sets he'd built for her fucking play. He'd never get past her walls. She'd made it clear: she wasn't interested in pursuing their friendship or mutual attraction.

He took deep gulps of air, trying to calm down, and got in his truck. He was still on the clock, but he'd be damned if he went back in until he was sure she was out of the auditorium. He went to the big box hardware store where the Durango had a charge account and bought enough wood and paint to finish the set. When he returned to the theater, the stage was deserted. His hands weren't trembling anymore, and he picked up the big pencil and went back to work on the tombstones.

As the afternoon passed and the tombstones took shape, his anger faded and disappointment moved in. She was never going to give him a fair shake. She was determined to hold his past against him. He knew sooner or later her attitude was going to rub off on the rest of the Durango staff. They'd been friendly enough to him so far, probably because they owed Miguel a favor and they knew it. But they weren't going to feel beholden to Miguel forever, and Rachel's negativity was going to infect everyone else. She'd already trash-mouthed him more than once. She'd do it again in a heartbeat, and given her deep-seeded need to be right even in the face of extenuating circumstances, she'd work hard to sway everyone to her way of thinking.

Shit. His days at the Durango were numbered.

He finished the tombstones and checked the time. He'd put in a full day and then some, so he headed over to his sister's place. But going to her crowded little house didn't appeal, so instead, he turned around and went to the small lake a few blocks from the theater where he parked his ass on a bench and watched the joggers trot by in the last rays of the setting sun.

He didn't know what the hell to do. If he stayed at the Durango, he'd have to work with Rachel. He'd have to put up with her overt hostility and her barbed comments, biding his time while she undermined his position until the rest of the staff felt the same way she did. All while trying to forget the fuckin' amazing kiss they shared, and forcing himself to ignore the attraction he felt for her despite her asshole attitude toward him.

He wasn't sure he had it in him to do it.

Maybe he would be better off working for Miguel full time. He wouldn't have the opportunity to exercise his creativity while installing cabinets and framing new houses, but he'd be away from Rachel. He wouldn't have to put up with her contempt or watch her undermine his job. He wouldn't have to be around her, wanting a woman who considered him the scum of the earth and who'd never lower herself to associate with him. He was already working for Miguel some, and while he would hardly consider his coworkers there his friends, at least they weren't out and out hostile.

He could do a lot worse than working for Abonce Construction full time.

He scrolled down to Miguel's number and punched it. At first he thought it was going to voice mail, but on the last ring Miguel answered. "Harlan. How's it goin'? What can I do for you, *amigo*?"

Harlan took a deep breath. "Things aren't going all that well at the Durango. Is there any way you could take me on full time?"

Chapter Seven

Rachel

Rachel wandered into the kitchen and rubbed her sleepy eyes at the sight of Felicia standing in front of the Keurig loading a pile of leftover party food onto a paper plate. "Well, good morning, Pocahontas. I didn't think you'd be up this early given how late we went to bed last night."

"I'm still on Eastern Time. The party was a success or what?"

Their mother's birthday party had run into the wee hours of the morning. "Yep. I would've thought at their ages, her friends would have gone nighty-night a lot earlier than they stumbled out of here."

"They're all retired and don't have to get up and be anywhere. Must be nice."

"Aw come on, you love your job. Whatever it is."

Felicia grinned mysteriously. "I'll never tell."

And she wouldn't. Felicia was employed by a shadowy government agency and was loosely based at Fort Sam, but she worked all over the world, doing things so hush-hush her own family knew next to nothing about it. She spent over eighty percent of her time somewhere other than in San Antonio and made an art form of living out of a suitcase. She'd missed more than one family celebration over the years, and Rachel had been surprised when Felicia showed up for this one.

"You gonna be around for a few days this time?"

"I fly out this afternoon."

"No time to see Edwin. That's a shame." Felicia had been going out with a fellow government employee for the last year or so. Edwin Purcell was a few years older than Felicia and had a teenage son, and from her typical smile at the mention of him, Rachel suspected her sister thought a lot of the man.

But that smile was noticeably absent this morning. "No, I didn't have time," she said tersely. "I wouldn't have seen him anyway. Edwin and I have come to a parting of the ways." Rachel was surprised. "He's not the man he ought to be."

"What? But I thought—"

Felicia held up her hand. "It's better you don't know."

"Well, hell. Another Castillo sister strikes out in the game of romance."

"The usual Castillo luck." Felicia's lips twisted bitterly.

"You got it. Amy's sleazeball ex is out of jail and trying to pick up where they left off."

"Leshawn? Well, shit. Don't tell me she went back to that motherfucker."

"No, she has better sense these days, but he's texted her several times and came around once. I don't think he's done bothering her."

"Well shit." Felicia shook her head. "And you? I'm certain you don't have any Leshawns lurking about."

"Don't be so sure. The other day I was every bit as stupid as Amy."

"I doubt it."

"No, really. I let our set designer, who the theater never should've hired in the first place, kiss the hell out of me. He got mad yesterday when I told him it was a mistake and there would be no repeats."

"Why was it a mistake? Why won't there be repeats?"

"He's an ex-con. He spent nearly ten years behind bars for murder."

Felicia sucked in a breath. "Well, hell. What's the story? Why'd he do it?"

"Don't know and don't care."

"I see. Why'd they hire him?"

"Miguel asked them to and they couldn't turn him down."

Felicia was silent. "There has to be more to it or they wouldn't've hired him. They're not so beholden to Miguel they'd hire a dangerous man. If I were you, I'd look it up and see."

"The bottom line is he killed somebody. Case closed."

Felicia tilted her head and squinted her eyes. "If you say so."

"Anyway, I'm sorry about Edwin."

Felicia's face shuttered. "So am I."

Rachel swallowed the rest of her coffee and headed out the door. Damn. She'd hoped Felicia had finally caught a break in the romance department. Her sister's ex-husband wasn't in Leshawn's league, but he was no prize either. It didn't look like any of the Castillo sisters were going to win the dating game any time soon, if ever.

The theater was deserted when Rachel arrived. She spent the morning going through contracts and noting the clauses she wanted their attorney Eli Solomon to look over. She started to walk to the Fruteria for lunch, but changed her mind and went the other direction to order a take-out tray of buffalo wings at Thirties. Despite all the party food, she was hungry. At least it's what she told herself. She wasn't about to admit she was avoiding the Fruteria because it held memories of her delightful afternoon in Harlan's company or the wild kiss they'd shared. She *would not* let herself remember how wonderful it was. Better to focus on the bitter argument they'd had yesterday afternoon, otherwise, it'd be too tempting to give in and let him into her life.

She had finished the last of the sticky, spicy buffalo wings and was looking over tryout applications for the upcoming January/February production of *American Idiot* when her phone rang. She glanced at the name and smiled. "What can I do for you, Cameron?"

"Meet me in the conference room. Now."

Rachel bristled at his tone. What the hell crawled up his ass?

She put the applications to one side and walked down the hall to the conference room, which doubled as a breakroom. Cameron and

Josh were seated at the table. Josh's arms were folded in front of him and Cameron was gripping the arms of his chair. He let go long enough to gesture to the empty chair at the end of the table. They both looked like they'd swallowed a pickle.

Rachel ignored the alarm bells going off in her head and sat. She folded her hands in front of her and looked Cameron in the eye without speaking. He and Josh looked at one another and Josh nodded to Cameron. "We got a phone call from Miguel this morning. He's an unhappy man. And so are we."

"What about?"

"Harlan," Cameron snapped. "Apparently you and he had words yesterday afternoon."

Her lips tightened. "So Harlan went whining to Miguel. Big whoop."

"Yeah, it's a damn big whoop." Cameron's knuckles whitened on the chair. "You not only pissed off our biggest benefactor, but you're also about to cost us the best set designer we ever had."

"What do you mean?" she asked having a niggling feeling in her stomach.

"I showed Cam the *Addams Family* set," Josh said. "It's the best set we've ever had. It's fantastic. Genius. And even though we talked about this and I told you we know all about Harlan's background, you managed to alienate him. He went to Miguel and asked for a full-time job at Abonce Construction. He doesn't feel welcome here. He's convinced you're going to undermine his position until we listen to you and fire him." Josh glared across the table.

"Harlan didn't go whining to Miguel." Cameron added. "He asked for another job. Miguel said it took an hour and three beers to get the story out of him."

"He didn't get the entire story out of him, or we wouldn't be here," Rachel said tersely. "Harlan got pissed when I wouldn't go out with him after I told him kissing him was a mistake I didn't intend to repeat." She felt her face flame. "Or is it now in my job description I have to date ex-con set designers to keep them happy?"

Cameron's jaw dropped, and Josh's eyes widened. "You kissed him?" he squeaked.

"Not one of my proudest moments," she admitted.

Cameron and Josh looked at one another. "Miguel didn't say anything about that. I have no idea if Harlan told him," Cameron said. "So you kissed him and had second thoughts. Fair enough. But what about the rest? Miguel said your remarks went a lot further than turning him down flat. Some of them border on harassment."

"But pestering me for a date isn't? The harassment business works two ways, Cameron. Don't throw the accusation around unless you're ready to have it thrown back."

"Okay. Calm down, both of you," Josh said. "Nobody's accusing anyone of harassment. But we need to know what you said. Harlan's convinced your opinion of him undermines his job at the Durango."

"Like I could do that." She was so pissed off she didn't know how she kept from screaming. "I didn't say anything I haven't said before. And I'll say it again. I don't know what the two of you and Miguel were thinking hiring an ex-con, a murderer no less, to work at the Durango. He has no business here, and I wish to hell you never hired him in the first place. I don't care how much we owe Miguel. A man like him killed Daddy. Damn it, I'm not trying to be mean. It scares me having him here."

"A man like Harlan didn't kill your father," Cameron said shaking his head like he was dealing with a recalcitrant child. "And Harlan is not a dangerous man." He turned to Josh. "You didn't explain it to her?"

"I told her to Google it. Miss Hardhead refuses. She's convinced the circumstances surrounding his case don't matter."

"They don't," Rachel said firmly.

"Wrong," Cameron ground out. "I remember everything about the case. At the time, I told my mother they should've pinned a medal on his chest."

"What the hell is wrong with you people? He killed a man," Rachel shouted.

"A man who needed to die," Josh said. "Which you'd know, if you weren't so damned narrowminded."

"I'm not narrowminded. Things like this fall under right and wrong," she said defensively.

"Textbook definition of narrowminded." Cameron looked her in the eye. "Things in this world are seldom as cut and dried as you'd like them to be. There are lots of nuanced situations, this being one of them. At the risk of pissing you off even more, I'm gonna admit, I'm seriously disappointed in you. Prejudice is an ugly thing, Rachel. Ugly and unfair. You as a woman of color should know that deep in your bones."

"It's not the same," she said hotly. "Racial prejudice is one thing. My feeling about Harlan and other criminals is something else entirely."

Cameron and Josh both pinned her with their gazes. "No, it's not," Josh said softly.

"It's entirely the same," Cameron added. "You're refusing to look past what you think a murderer is and see the person and the circumstances behind it. If that isn't prejudice, I don't know what is."

"You don't like it when people don't look past the color of your skin, and you get downright indignant when someone judges Cam and me for being gay. But you're doing the same thing to Harlan. You're judging him on his criminal record. How is that different? How is it okay?" Josh asked.

"What am I supposed to do? Forget that a criminal murdered Daddy? Pretend Harlan's like the rest of us?" Rachel cried. "Go out with him to keep him happy?"

"You're supposed to do what I told you to," Josh said. "You're supposed to get over yourself and find out why Harlan did what he did so you can work with him like a decent human being."

"You're under no obligation to date him or see him socially, but you have every obligation to treat him professionally," Cameron added. "As your boss, I'm going to pull rank. You made this mess. You make it right."

"How do you expect me to do that?" she asked tightly.

"You can start by going online tonight and reading up on his case. Will the honor system work, or do I need a written report tomorrow?" Cameron jabbed.

Rachel's face burned. "Honor system's fine."

"Then you need to talk to Harlan," Cam continued. "He needs to know you'll treat him with the same respect you do the rest of us."

"And if he comes on to me again?" she asked.

"Do you really think he'd want to go out with you?" Josh asked dryly.

"If it becomes a problem, we'll deal," Cameron said.

"Anything else?" she asked through gritted teeth.

"Yep. I'm having Harlan work the lights for *The Addams Family*," Josh said. "Tikia doesn't want to commit to doing a show during the holidays. Most of his interaction will be with Miranda, not you, but you'll have to work with him some. We need you to do it in a professional manner. Got me?"

"Fine," she said quietly.

Cameron sighed. "Rachel, we understand why you feel like you do. A violent criminal robbed your father of his life and you and your sisters of a father. You have every right to your feelings about violent criminals. But Harlan's not violent. He did what he did because he was between a rock and a hard place and didn't feel he had a choice in the matter. He paid dearly for it and he deserves a second chance."

"And here at the Durango we're all about acceptance and giving people second chances," Josh added. "We need you to you find it in yourself to accept him as we do everyone."

Rachel was quiet for a moment. "I'll try. That's all I can promise."

"Google him. Find out what really happened. You'll be able to do more than try," Cameron said encouragingly. "I guarantee it."

Chapter Eight

Rachel

Rachel sat in the sunroom and stared at the computer screen of her laptop. She still didn't think anything would change her mind about Harlan, but Cameron had made it clear: she needed to find out exactly what had gone down to make Harlan think he had to murder a man so she could find it in herself to accept him working at the theater. She'd held on to her indignation throughout most of the discussion with Josh and Cameron, but they'd finally gotten through to her with the reminder the Durango was all about acceptance. They were right. Among its other virtues, the theater was a haven for people who didn't feel they had a place elsewhere. Including her sister. Amy had lost most of her friends when she'd gotten involved with Leshawn, and the rest of her social circle when she lost her job. The Durango crowd had welcomed her with open arms, for which Rachel was grateful.

They expected her to do the same for Harlan. She wasn't sure she could. But Josh and Cameron seemed to think knowing what happened would make a difference, so here she was. She took a deep breath and typed in his name. Dozens of links appeared, several pages in fact. The first was dated 2011.

Soldier Arrested in Abuser's Murder.

The second line read: **Sister Still Hospitalized.**

Rachel's eyes widened. What abuser? Whose sister was still hospitalized? She clicked on the link.

Cpl. Harlan Burke, currently stationed at Fort Hood, was arrested this morning for the murder of San Antonio resident Cole Abernathy. Abernathy was gunned down last evening at his home at

5577 Morning Chase after an altercation with Cpl. Burke over Abernathy's alleged abuse of Burke's sister. Carrie Burke was found unconscious earlier in the day and is listed in serious condition at the Medical Center. Ms. Burke and Abernathy's children were taken into custody by Child Protective Services. Cpl. Burke is in the Bexar County Jail awaiting arraignment on charges of murder.

Rachel stared at the laptop screen in shock. He'd killed his sister's abuser. Of all the scenarios she'd imagined, it was the last one she'd have come up with.

She finished reading through the article and moved to the next link.

Soldier Pleads Not Guilty to Murdering Alleged Abuser, Claims Defense of Sister.

The next was a detailed description of the arraignment. There were multiple links to newspaper articles and television news features reporting on the case in salacious detail, along with several op ed pieces and any number of letters to the editor. Social media had a field day, with some taking a law-and-order position, but many more sympathizing with Harlan.

Dude did what he had to do.

That tweet went viral, as did several social media posts to the same effect.

Rachel kept searching. The trial was covered in gory detail by all the media outlets. All the usual suspects weighed in. The Medical Examiner testified as to the cause of death: a gunshot wound through the heart at close range.

Witnesses for the prosecution testified to seeing Harlan ring Abernathy's doorbell and shoot him point-blank with a forty-four magnum. The owner of the gun shop admitted to selling Harlan the gun and the ammunition the afternoon of the shooting, a full three hours before Abernathy was gunned down. By the time the prosecution rested its case, there was no doubt as to what had happened. Upon hearing Abernathy had put his sister in the hospital,

Harlan had thought about it for a couple of hours and then gone out, purchased a lethal weapon, and shot Cole Abernathy dead.

But that wasn't the entire story. Rachel read on.

Harlan's attorneys mounted a vigorous defense. Witness after witness testified as to Abernathy's long history of abusing Harlan's sister. Carrie Burke had been terrified of the man despite a five-year relationship, which included having two children together. The police had responded to call after call. He was finally put away for a short time, but the minute he was out the abuse resumed.

Carrie's mother and stepfather described Abernathy's abominable treatment of their daughter, admitting they were afraid of him as well. Carrie had taken the stand, her testimony moving some of the women jurors to tears as she described being terrified for her life, and for the lives of her children should he ever obtain custody of them. Abernathy's wealthy parents insisted Cole was a "good boy" but were forced to admit under cross examination he'd been asked to move out of their house after severely beating his younger brother.

While Harlan never took the stand, the defense painted the picture of a young man terrified for his sister's life and helpless in the face of an ineffective law enforcement and judicial system.

Harlan believed he had no choice but to do what he did. Character witnesses ranged from his commanding officer in the Army to his old high school counselor, and they all assured the court Harlan wasn't out of control or violent. Far from it. The defense argued Harlan felt he had no other choice. He'd done what he felt he had to do to protect his sister and her children.

The jury bought it, but only to a point. The judge sentenced to ten years, the least amount of time the statute allowed, and Harlan had served seven of them. He'd been held accountable for his actions.

But a lot of people thought even the light sentence was too much, and said so in another social media storm.

Rachel read on. Once the trial was over, the case continued to receive press. *Texas Monthly* had written an in-depth account of the crime and the circumstances surrounding it, in which law enforcement insisted they'd done all they could, and the Abernathys staunchly defended their son and said he'd been a helpless victim to Harlan's rage.

Harlan described in detail his emotions the day of the murder. "The justice system wasn't going to do anything," he said bitterly in a prison interview. "They picked him up in the morning and he was out by noon. His daddy's lawyer saw to that. If I hadn't done what I did, I honestly believed he would've walked in the hospital and finished what he'd started."

"Do you regret killing him?" the interviewer had asked.

"I regret having to. If the system had taken care of things, I wouldn't be sitting here today."

Rachel read through the in-depth article twice. There wasn't much more written after its publication. The *Texas Monthly* article was the last major coverage Harlan's case generated and his release had gone unnoticed. The media had gone on to fresh stories and Cole Abernathy's murder had been mostly forgotten.

Except by the two families shattered by the tragedy.

Rachel sat deep in thought as the sun sank and the sky darkened. What she'd learned explained a lot. To Harlan's friends, he had sacrificed years of his life and the future he'd dreamed of to save his sister, which made him a hero. Miguel most likely felt the same, which was why he'd gone out of his way to help Harlan. Cameron and Josh both expressed the contempt many felt for Harlan's victim. She had no idea what the rest of the Durango staff thought, but however they felt, they were accepting of the man. Since he wasn't typically a violent person, no one had any reason to fear him, or to be wary of him.

No one else wanted him gone from the theater.

He wasn't like the violent criminal who'd taken her father's life. Harlan wouldn't murder a policeman over a broken taillight. She was certain of it.

But she still had her reservations.

Had it been necessary to take Abernathy's life? She didn't know. She'd read the articles carefully, trying to parse out opinion and mine the facts. But some facts were elusive, buried in the avalanche of speculation. Such as why it took repeated calls before Abernathy was finally arrested. Why, when he was arrested and tried, he spent so little time behind bars? And why Carrie had consistently refused to testify against him. Harlan had felt he had no choice but to turn to murder. Surely someone could've done something to avert a heartbreaking tragedy.

But nobody had. Abernathy had died, and Harlan had paid the price for taking his life.

She felt bad for Harlan. To feel like his only choice was to commit murder. It hadn't been, she was certain of it, but he must have felt like it was. Still, a man had died at his hands.

Rachel was still sitting in the sunroom when the front door opened and Amy appeared a couple of minutes later. "Sitting out here communing with nature?" she teased as she flopped down on the other lounge chair.

"Sort of. Did you know Harlan went to prison for killing his sister's abuser?"

"Uh-uh. No, wait a minute. Nine or ten years ago. Fort Hood soldier blew the boyfriend away after the boyfriend damn near killed his sister. Yeah, I remember it. Media circus for months."

"That's it. Why don't I remember anything about it?"

"Check the dates. You were still in New York." Rachel had gone to drama school at NYU and stayed a couple of years after graduation.

She checked the dates. "Yeah, I was. I moved back after it'd all died down."

"I didn't realize it was him. How long did he have to serve?"

"Seven years, not counting the time before the trial. He lost almost ten years of his life."

"Pretty damned unfair, if you ask me. He should've gotten a slap on the wrist."

"He did get a slap on the wrist, considering what he did. It's not like he snapped in a moment of fear or anger. He went out and bought the damned gun. He had an entire afternoon to change his mind and he didn't."

"He did what he thought he had to do. Maybe he had to. You know as well as I do the system's rigged against the victim." Amy's mouth twisted bitterly.

Rachel looked over at her sister. "We're not talking about Harlan anymore, are we?"

"No, we aren't. Leshawn texted me again. Insists we need to get back together. And he drove by the house this morning after you left. He made damn sure I saw him."

"Did you call the cops?"

"Why bother? Besides, he didn't threaten me. Except you and I both know the fact that he's driving by and texting does constitute a threat."

"You need to call 'em anyway. We have laws against stalking, which is what he's doing. Get it on record even if you don't press charges."

"If it keeps up I will," Amy stated. "I know you don't want to hear it, but a big part of me thinks Harlan had to kill the bastard. If his sister was lying in a hospital bed beat to hell and the bastard was out four hours later. It makes me think faulting Harlan isn't right."

"You and everyone else in the world," Rachel murmured.

"More of those shades of gray you don't agree with." She leaned forward and patted Rachel's leg as if to say *Poor thing, you haven't caught on yet.* "On another note, I'm hungry. Want me to hit the new Hawaiian place for some takeout? I could use a plate of kalua pork about now."

"Works for me. Katsu chicken would be great."

Amy got Rachel's order and sailed out the front door. Rachel was deep in thought as she put away her laptop. Despite the circumstances, she still thought what Harlan did was wrong. But she was relieved to learn he wasn't anything like the violent man who'd taken her father's life. Knowing what she did, she could see herself interacting with him pleasantly in a work situation. But that was all.

Getting involved with him was out of the question. He could be a valued colleague, nothing more. She would learn to ignore the powerful attraction she had for him and make herself forget how wonderful she had felt in his arms. She'd force herself to forget the most wonderful kiss she'd ever had in her life.

If she could.

***

Rachel stood in the back of the auditorium and watched as Harlan painted in the tombstones on the back wall of the set. The only lights were those on the stage, so it was unlikely he was aware of her presence. She tried to think about what to say, but the words stuck in the roof of her mouth. She owed him an apology. She needed to reassure him she was happy to work with him and wasn't gunning for his job.

At the same time, she needed to make it clear anything more than a professional relationship was off the table. In retrospect, she could understand why he'd thought she would be interested in more. She'd returned his kiss with equal passion, and that was on her. But he should've taken her refusal with good grace instead of pushing her. She didn't know if Josh or Cameron had talked to him about it yet. If they hadn't, she guessed it was up to her to explain that as well.

She wasn't looking forward to the upcoming conversation.

Rachel watched him for a few more minutes. He had on an old, tight t-shirt that'd seen better days. She watched his back muscles flex as he moved the paint brush over the tombstones, covering them with a base layer of a grayish white he probably would shade in later.

Damn. Those muscles had felt so good under her fingers, and a part of her itched to feel them there again. Which made this so unbelievably difficult. There was something powerful going on between them. The mutual attraction was off the charts, and under other circumstances she would've welcomed it. Reveled in it. Licked it up like dripping ice cream.

But no. She had to turn her back on it, ignore the sparks every time they came within ten feet of one another. It was up to her to keep their relationship strictly professional. She stretched her lips, having realized they were pursed and her brows were scrunched together. Sometimes having things black or white sucked royally.

She made her way down the side aisle and up the steps to the stage. Harlan turned and his face tensed when he spotted her. He stood up and waited for her to speak, his fists clenched at his side. "I'm sorry," she blurted, all her mental rehearsals going out the window. "I'm sorry I made you feel you had to quit. You're good at what you do and we wouldn't want to lose you."

Harlan stared at her. His blank expression unreadable. "I mean it. I should've never said the things I did," she went on. "The Durango's all about acceptance. I kind of forgot that for a while." He continued to stare. "Anyway, I'm sorry and I hope you won't quit."

"Whatever." He turned back to the unpainted set.

Whatever? That was all he had to say?

Frankly, she didn't know what she expected him to say, but whatever didn't seem to cover everything that'd happened.

She turned to go. Then dug in. They would get it all out in the open. "Look, I really am sorry." She stomped across the stage to within six feet of him. "Cam and Josh are right. You're the best set designer we've ever had." She took a breath. "But you pushed me. I'd told you 'no' and you wouldn't take 'no' for an answer."

He turned around, his eyes blazing. "Shame on me. I thought we had something nice going on. Believe me, I won't be making the same mistake again. I'll be a lot more careful who I *share* a kiss with from now on."

Rachel felt her face flame. "I realize I screwed up. I sent you mixed signals."

"Ya think?"

"Damn Harlan, I said I'm sorry. I'm trying to explain. I love your work and I'm more than happy to work with you as a set designer, and later when you're on the lights. But that's all. I don't want anything personal."

"Not a problem. Josh took me aside this morning and explained to me the error of my ways. I won't be trying it on with you anymore. Not that I would've anyway." He looked at her with undisguised disdain. "Believe me, you're the last woman I have any desire to go out with."

Rachel sucked in a breath. Damned if his honesty didn't sting like a wasp bite. "We're on the same page, then. Have a nice day."

She was almost to the stairs when he called her name. "Yeah?" She turned.

"Did you ever bother to look it up? Find out what happened?"

"I did."

He held her gaze for a moment. "And I'm still a violent criminal in your eyes, aren't I?"

"No, of course not. You did what you thought you had to do."

He shook his head. "I didn't do what I *thought* I had to do. I did what I *had* to do. Big difference."

She looked at him uncertain if she should tell him how she really felt. "But surely there was another answer. Surely something else could've been done."

"Jesus, Rachel. Do you think I would have deliberately gone out and bought a gun and shot a man in cold blood if there was another answer? Do you think I would've done something I knew would land my ass in jail for God knows how many years if something else could've been done'? Get real. I did what I had to do. If you don't like it, tough shit."

He turned his back and picked up his paint brush.

She made her way back to her office. That was almost as fucked-up as the last time they shouted at each other. She'd hurt him twice, and knowing it felt like shit. But still. Even though he'd acted for the noblest of reasons, he'd taken a man's life. Despite what he said, surely there had been another way to deal with his sister's abuser. Even if she had no idea what that might've been.

And, the worst part of all of this: she found him as appealing as ever.

Chapter Nine

Harlan

Harlan and Carrie walked out of the vacant apartment and shut the door behind them. "Another bust," he said as they headed to her car.

"I guess you're gonna have to pay more," Carrie said.

"They're already asking me to pay through the nose. And those are the ones who'll even talk to me. Most of them emailed 'Thanks but no thanks' after they did a background check." It had come as a rude shock to learn antidiscrimination laws didn't apply to criminal records. Leasing companies could and routinely did turn down convicted felons. So far only five complexes had been willing to show him apartments. They'd looked at four of the apartments already, and none of them were anyplace he'd want to live.

"We've got one more to look at. Who knows? It might be exactly what you're looking for."

"And I might be right back to square one. I may as well go on home."

"Not gonna know unless you try," Carrie stated. "Load in the address and we'll find out."

He glanced over at his sister. She'd changed while he was away. Before, she would've agreed with him and gone home.

Harlan entered the address into his phone's GPS. They drove halfway across town to a pleasant older neighborhood that wasn't too far from the theater, although it was outside the Deco District. Carrie parked in front of a comfortable-looking ranch house. "This has to be a mistake," Harlan said. "I don't see an apartment."

"Maybe not. There's a driveway going to the back of the house. They might have a garage apartment."

Harlan's eyebrow shot up. "And you would know this because?"

"The kids and I lived in one for a while."

Harlan thought of the three of them crammed in a tiny apartment and scowled. "I didn't realize."

"I told Mom and Joe not to tell you. It would've only made you worry."

Harlan took another look at the house. "You may as well drive on. No way is someone in a classy house like this going to be willing to rent to me."

"Nope, not gonna do it. They didn't bounce your application. For crying out loud, ring the doorbell and ask. All they can do is turn you down."

He heaved a heavy sigh. "If you say so."

They walked up to the front door and he braced. The doorbell reverberated through the house. *Here goes nothing.* They waited a minute and were about to ring a second time when the door flew open and the biggest, burliest, ugliest man he'd ever seen in his life looked down at the two of them. He wore an MC club tee shirt that'd seen better days, frayed jeans, and rundown Huaraches. His beard was grizzled and red dreadlocks liberally sprinkled with gray peeked out from under his do rag. His arms and neck were covered with tattoos, a couple of which Harlan recognized as the prison tats he'd foregone during his years behind bars.

Oh, shit.

The man looked him in the eye. "May I help you?" he asked gruffly.

"I... I—"

Carrie elbowed him. "My brother's here about the apartment you have for rent."

The man's eyes narrowed. "You the ex-con?"

Harlan nodded. *Like this dude had any reason to talk.*

"Whatja get sent up for?"

Harlan stiffened. "Never mind." He turned to go.

"Oh, no you don't." Carrie grabbed Harlan's hand. She turned to the man and stuck out her jaw. "He got sent up for shooting the man who nearly beat me to death," she said.

Wow. His sister had changed a fuckofalot while he was away. She would've never stuck up for him like that before.

"Oh." The man looked from him to her.

At that moment a pretty young woman carrying a tiny baby came to the door. She smiled at Harlan and Carrie, and thrust the baby toward the man. "Here, Red, take your cranky daughter and let me talk to these folks." She turned to Harlan and Carrie. "I'm Dottie Myers and this is my husband the Reverend Jerome 'Big Red' Myers. He's in a mood because he spent half the night bailing out one of his flock from jail and the other half with an unhappy baby."

Harlan's jaw nearly hit the ground. He never in his life had seen anyone less preacher-like.

Reverend Myers cradled the baby in one arm and stuck out his other hand. "Glad to meet ya." His lips held the barest of smiles.

"Likewise, Reverend," Harlan murmured.

"No formalities, please. Red will do. So you're here about the apartment. Come on around."

The four of them walked around the house to a detached two car garage with stairs going up to a second floor. Dottie unlocked the door and they stepped inside. Not bad, Harlan thought as he took in the studio apartment.

The main room doubled as the bedroom, with a faux-leather futon that folded down into a double bed with a chair on either side. The futon and chairs faced an entertainment console big enough to hold whatever electronics the renter brought with them.

An efficiency kitchen lined one wall, with an apartment-sized stove and refrigerator, and a window in front of the sink. A small dining table sat to one side.

Two doors on another wall stood slightly ajar, one of which led to a small, but adequate bathroom, and the other to a surprisingly roomy closet. He sat on the futon and bounced once. Comfortable enough. He looked around the apartment. Nothing fancy, far from it. But it was clean and the paint job was fairly recent. Most important, there would be no cellmate snoring four feet from him or teenage nephew in the next bed.

For the first time in nearly ten years, he could be alone.

Red, Dottie, and Carrie looked at him. "I like it," he said. He turned to the couple. "I'm sure you have some questions for me."

Red looked him up and down. "A few. So you shot your sister's abuser. Ever in trouble before then?"

"No, sir."

"No drugs, bar fights, arrests of any kind?"

"None."

"Your application said you work down the way at the theater."

Harlan nodded. "And some for Abonce Construction when the theater doesn't need me."

Dottie and Red glanced at one another and Dottie cleared her throat. "Okay, then. Here's the deal. There were some folks who stepped up and helped Red when he first got out and we try to do the same. But you have to keep your nose clean if you want to live here. Stay on the right side of the law. Sounds like you're doing it already, so I don't see a problem. Oh. No parties and no hell-raising. The neighbors are mostly elderly and go to bed early. So do we when we can." She told him the rent, which was reasonable. "Come back tomorrow and we'll have a lease ready for you to sign."

"Thank you." Harlan smiled at her. "When can I move in?"

"Tomorrow if you like. We can pro-rate your first month. One more thing." She smiled mischievously. "It's certainly not part of living here or anything, but Red's church is a couple of blocks down the way and we'd love to have you join us for services."

Harlan nodded noncommittally. He and God had gotten crossways when Abernathy was abusing Carrie. Harlan hadn't come to terms with Him yet.

He thanked them again and he and Carrie headed for her place.

"A minister?" She laughed. "I never met anyone less like a preacher in my life."

"Probably a prison conversion. Those aren't usually genuine, but his must've been."

"Whatever." Carrie was as soured on religion as he was. "Anyway, I'm assuming you want to go back to the house and pack. Tonight's burgers and all the fixin's cooked out on the grill. We're celebrating your new place."

"And getting me out of yours," he said dryly.

"Well, yeah. How else are you ever gonna have a social life? You know, dating and booty calls, and all such fun. It's about time you had a little action with the opposite sex."

Rachel's disapproving expression flashed in front of his face. "Like that's gonna happen anytime soon."

"Why not?" Carrie stopped for a red light. "You've now got a place to take a lady."

"It's not gonna impress a lady."

"It's better than a lot of people have. You can drive them in your chariot." She winked.

"Don't you mean in the truck from hell?"

"New wheels are next. Besides, nowadays, the lady probably has her own transportation."

He thought of Rachel's Charger. "Yeah, she does," he said dryly.

"Yeah, who does?" Carrie pounced like a cat on a mouse.

"Nobody," he said quickly.

"I'm calling bullshit. *Who,* Harlan?"

"She works at the theater," Harlan said slowly.

"Do you see her often? Is she nice? Does she want to go out with you?"

"No, I don't see her often." He'd hardly seen her at all since their set-to last month. He knew she was around, but she never came into the auditorium while he was there working, and he sure as hell hadn't sought her out. She'd sent him an email when *The Addams Family* sets were done telling him she liked them, so she must've seen them while he wasn't there. He'd done a few more projects at the theater and their usual lighting technician had spent a couple afternoons training him, but the last couple of weeks he had spent most of his time at Miguel's construction sites. Which in some ways was a relief: there was no possibility of running into her at a construction site.

Even if another part of him missed her.

Especially the kissing her part.

"Well?" Carrie prompted.

"Well, what?"

"I asked you if she was nice and if she wanted to go out with you."

"She's mostly nice, but she sure as hell doesn't want to go out with me."

"And you know this because? Have you even tried to ask her out?"

Harlan sighed. "Because I tried and it blew up in my face. We had the fight from hell and we both got into trouble with management. Her for telling me I had no business working at the theater because of my record and me for asking her to go out with me after she'd turned me down." He started to mention the kiss but decided there were some things Carrie didn't need to know.

"Any reason she's so vehement?"

"Huge one. Her dad was a cop. An ex-con murdered him at a traffic stop. She's bitter."

"Does she know what really happened?" Carrie asked softly. "With you and Cole?"

"She does now, after the boss made her look it up. But it really doesn't make any difference. She came out with the usual 'there had to be another way' crap and didn't appear to like it when I set her straight."

"Okay. This woman—"

"Rachel."

"Okay, Rachel's out. But there must be other ladies, nice ones who aren't going to hold what you did against you. Maybe you should stop mooning about this Rachel person and get out there and find one."

Yeah, right. Like he could do that when he was still interested in Rachel despite everything that'd gone down.

Carrie reached out and took his hand. "You're forgetting something. Our friends, the people who really matter, are firmly in your corner. A lot of the rest of the world is as well. You need to stop brooding about Rachel and the others like her, and get on with rebuilding your life. Which includes finding a lady friend. Or several of them." She squeezed his hand before letting go. "The first step is to celebrate with burgers and get you packed up for your move tomorrow. Right?"

"Right." He'd do it. Get moved and get on with his life.

And try his damnedest to forget how wonderful Rachel felt in his arms.

Chapter Ten

Rachel

A brisk November wind buffeted Rachel as she locked the front door and sprinted to her car, where Amy waited in the passenger seat. The first norther had blown in the night before, cooling the air and inspiring locals to dig out a sweatshirt or cardigan or two, even though it would be warm again in a couple of days. Amy glanced around furtively as Rachel started the engine. "Do you see him?" she asked as Rachel backed out of the driveway.

"No, but then I haven't looked for him." Rachel's hands tightened on the wheel. "Did you see him or something?"

"Not today."

Rachel looked both ways before backing out of the driveway. She didn't see Leshawn's Lexus, or any other cars that were out of place. "How long has it been since he drove down the street?"

"Nearly a week since I actually saw him. But he left another phone message this morning. Who knows how often he drives by while I'm at work."

"Shit." Rachel turned onto the street leading out of their subdivision. Still no evidence of Leshawn this evening. She breathed a little easier as she made her way onto Austin Highway. "How many phone messages now?"

"Three. And another four texts. He's been leaving about one a week." She held up her hands. "I know, I know, you want me to call the police again," she said when Rachel started to speak. "But I'm not sure he's breaking any laws."

"He's continuing to contact you when you've asked him not to. I'm not a lawyer, but I think it constitutes stalking. Even if he doesn't stop the car."

"If he keeps it up, I will."

"Save the texts and the phone messages. Or better yet, change phone numbers."

"No way. I've had this phone number for fifteen years and I have to give it up for a piece of shit like him? Besides, Granny will never remember a new one and she's too hardheaded to tape the number by the landline. Are we ever gonna persuade her to get a smartphone?"

"She doesn't even have a computer or cable. I wish *Abuela* would rub it in a little more." *Abuela* had Rachel's mom's old laptop and had mastered social media and spending money online, although she didn't do much else with it. "Anyway, if he keeps it up, you might not have a choice."

"He scares me. The way he won't take no for an answer."

It scared Rachel too.

She sped through the light Sunday afternoon traffic toward the theater. Today she had other concerns. Tech Week, the grueling week-long prelude to opening night, started today and would continue until the show opened on Friday, the day after Thanksgiving. Tried and true, the cast would assemble for their final dress rehearsal on Thanksgiving night, so Rachel and Amy's mother and grandmothers were serving their sumptuous dinner at noon. *Abuela* had grumbled a bit. "I'll have to get up at the crack of dawn," she'd groused.

"At least we'll be there. Felicia flew out again yesterday." Amy had made her point with a smile. Their sister had made it back to town for a couple of days but was already gone.

"Where'd she go this time?" *Abuela* demanded when she learned of Felicia's departure. "California? Europe? Timbuktu?"

Rachel and Amy had looked at one another and shrugged. They had no idea where she'd gone any more than *Abuela* did.

Rachel pulled into the parking lot and the two of them headed inside. Amy disappeared into the ladies' dressing room. The cast wouldn't rehearse in their costumes until tomorrow night, but the costumes had been delivered and Amy was eager to see her black, slinky Morticia dress. Rachel ducked into her office for her headset and then headed for the stage, passing Sasha coming up the side steps.

Rachel didn't know what to make of the quiet, uncommunicative girl. She was withdrawn in the extreme and had yet to warm up to anyone at the theater, much less join them at Thirties, but she was marvelous on the stage once the curtain went up. Her portrayal of Nellie Forbush in *South Pacific* had been spot on, and she brought to Wednesday Addams a quirky poignancy that lifted the character out of the usual cartoon portrayal and made her someone to cheer for.

Rachel motioned to Gina Rodriguez, an Academy alumnus from a few years back who was serving as her crew chief. The stage crew had been at it since ten this morning, spiking the stage with colored tape and marking off lines for every set piece appearing in every scene. Rachel and Gina went over the spiking. Rachel checked the placement of each piece carefully. Gina and the crew had done their job. The furniture would be placed correctly and there would be plenty of room for the actors to move around during the three dance numbers. Jessica had choreographed the dancing, which was uncomplicated enough for Rachel to direct.

Harlan had done his job as well. Rachel had already seen the finished set walls, as well as Gomez and Morticia's gothic headboard and the long skinny table that would be unfolded for the dinner scene. He'd also spent a couple of afternoons scouring antique stores for an old-fashioned sofa and fainting couch and had found the perfect pieces for the Addams living room. She gave herself a moment to appreciate the set he'd designed and built and to allow herself a moment of satisfaction.

It was the best set the Durango had ever had. Which was saying a lot, considering the marvelous sets from previous productions.

Harlan was hands down the most talented set designer she'd ever worked with.

It was a crying damned shame there was so much else that wasn't marvelous.

Rachel thanked Gina and moved to the back of the auditorium. Her stomach clenched when she spotted Harlan in Tikia's place behind the light board, standing beside their sound man Noah Humphries. Tikia had spent a couple of afternoons training Harlan and had given him an enthusiastic two thumbs up afterwards. "He caught on in a hot New York minute," she'd enthused. "You won't have a thing to worry about."

No, she wouldn't, which meant she could spend all her time remembering how wonderful kissing him had been. And how she wished she could kiss him again. She couldn't understand it. The set-to they'd had, and the trouble they'd both gotten into for it should've put her off him. So should the apology gone sour. Instead, she found herself more attracted to him than ever.

She'd relived the moments in his arms way too often and wished from the bottom of her heart his past wasn't what it was. Or that she'd been different. Plenty of women would've overlooked his criminal record and been delighted to go out with him. But she wasn't made that way.

While looking forward to Tech Week otherwise, she dreaded having to work with him, feeling the way she did.

She didn't have a choice, so she pushed those thoughts out of her head. Harlan and Noah had taped a list of notes to their consoles, although she doubted Noah would even need his by opening night. If Harlan was as sharp as Tikia insisted, he probably wouldn't either.

Miranda was already beside them with her clipboard in her hand. While Rachel was in charge this evening, their talented production manager would be learning the production from inside out and would step in at the first performance, assuming the actual management of the production. She was chatting easily with Harlan, both with big smiles on their faces. Harlan seemed relaxed, more so than she'd ever seen him: easy in his skin. He had begun to lose the wariness that'd been evident ever since he'd come to work at the theater.

Wariness she'd probably contributed to with her pissy attitude.

Miranda moved away and Harlan's gaze met Rachel's. His smile faded and he nodded his head. "Evenin'." His voice was polite, but his expression was cool.

She'd wondered if he'd softened any in the last month. It didn't look like it. He was still as pissed as ever.

Not that she blamed him.

"Evenin'." She made a point of including Noah in her greeting. "Have you gentlemen had a chance to meet?"

"We have." Noah made a production of looking Harlan up and down. "He's not as sexy as Tikia, but I guess he'll do."

Not as sexy? Guess it depends on who does the looking.

Harlan grimaced good-naturedly and Rachel made herself laugh at the joke. "So, are you gentlemen ready to go? As soon as the band and the cast are assembled, we're running through Amy and Eric's tango with the Addams ghosts. Let's see what kind of lighting you have for it."

Harlan flipped a couple of switches and the stage was bathed in an orange-tinted glow. "Perfect. Let's see the lights for the dinner scene."

Those were spot-on as well, as were the spooky outdoor scenes. Josh hadn't made a mistake moving Harlan to the light board. Unlike the actors, the technicians were paid for each performance, although not a great deal. Harlan could probably use the money.

His expression continued to be closed off. Not that it took away from his appeal, she thought as the actors began to assemble in the front rows of the auditorium.

Even though they were several feet apart, she could catch the faintest whiff of his soap and aftershave. It had felt so wonderful in his arms, right here in the back of the theater. She glanced over at him and wondered if he ever thought of that afternoon and their spectacular kiss.

She strode to the front of the auditorium. The cast assembled quickly and the musical director gave her a thumbs up from the balcony.

"Welcome to the first night of Dead Week. If you don't feel dead already, we guarantee you will by Friday evening."

The cast and crew laughed.

She went on with a brief welcoming speech to the crew and a thanks to the cast for the work they'd already put in. She also made a point to acknowledge the band. Too many directors took them for granted, and she was determined not to.

Then she gestured to the back of the auditorium. "As always, a thumbs up and a thanks to our sound and light men. Noah is coming back for his sixth or is it seventh show for us. This is Harlan's first show on the light board. We need to give him a hearty round of applause for taking us on." There. She could be gracious.

Harlan bobbed his head as the cast applauded politely. This far away, she couldn't see his expression clearly, but she doubted her acknowledgement had done much to blunt his resentment.

She acknowledged a couple of other contributions and then it was time to get down to business. They rehearsed the dance numbers first and as Amy and Eric glided around the stage in their sexy tango number, Rachel thanked her mom and dad for investing in dance lessons for the Castillo girls.

Amy nailed her other dance as well, as did the entire cast for the third dance. They ran through a couple of other numbers before going through the production once in its entirety. Rachel and Miranda sat side by side on the front row, each making copious notes as to what worked, what didn't, and where improvements needed to be made.

Rachel's awareness of Harlan took a back seat to the production going on in front of her, but to her immense aggravation it never went away entirely. Especially when the lighting changed. She'd have to get over it. She had a week of rehearsals to get through and the production would run through the Christmas season. Mooning over Harlan was going to get damned old if she didn't.

It was nearly ten before they had run through the play in its entirety. The cast and crew re-assembled in front with Harlan and Noah joining them for the postmortem. Between them, Rachel and Miranda filled almost an hour with observations and instructions. Finally, Rachel dismissed the cast with a reminder there would be another rehearsal at seven tomorrow evening and an admonition to please be on time. "Come straight from work and we'll order food from Thirties if we have to," she said.

"Easy for you," Letti teased. "You're already at work."

"You've never been late to a rehearsal in your life," Rachel teased back. "And when you direct you string up the tardies by their thumbs."

Everyone who'd ever been directed by Letti laughed out loud. Rachel dismissed the cast and crew, and the crew got to work righting the stage for rehearsal the next evening. The crew chief had a key to lock up, so she and Amy headed for the door.

"Good rehearsal. It's coming together wonderfully," Amy said.

"It is. By Friday it will be something else."

They stepped outside and Amy gripped Rachel's arm. "Over there. Leaning against your car," she whispered. "It's him."

Rachel peered out into the night. Leshawn lounged against the Charger smoking a cigarette. "Son of a bitch," she ground out. "It *is* him."

Amy looked at her, fear written all over Amy's face. "What do we do?"

"We either go in and call the cops or brazen it out."

Amy glanced around the parking lot. "If you tell them it's not an emergency, they'll be forever getting here and we'll be alone with him outside waiting for us. There are enough people here he won't do anything because he'll have witnesses. Come on." She took Rachel's arm and steered her toward the car.

Leshawn spotted them almost immediately. He straightened and threw his cigarette on the pavement, grinding it out with his heel. He'd changed, Rachel thought. Before, he'd been thin and wiry, and his face had held boyish charm. It looked like he'd put on a good thirty pounds since she'd seen him last, every bit of it muscle. His shoulders were broad under his tight t-shirt and his legs were thicker than they'd been. His face had lost any vestiges of boyishness and was hard, and his expression was sardonic as he turned to face them.

Rachel surmised the changes were courtesy of his years in the prison system. *Thank you, State of Texas.*

He looked Amy up and down insolently and then turned his attention to Rachel. "Well, well, well. If it isn't the Castillo girls. If you two aren't the finest lookin' two sistahs I've seen in a *dayum* long time." He leered at them and licked his lips.

Amy glared at him. "What are you doing here, Leshawn?" Rachel had to give her sister credit. She could feel Amy's hand trembling on her arm, but Amy looked cool and confident, and properly disdainful.

"You're trespassing on private property," Rachel added coldly.

Leshawn raised his hands. "A parking lot? Really?" he said smilingly. "Don't look so private to me."

"But it is. You are definitely trespassing, and I would be happy to call SAPD and tell them so," Rachel added.

Leshawn's smile faded. "Now why would you want to do that? All I want to do is talk to Amy here. She and I...we got a lot of catching up to do." He turned to Amy and smiled beguilingly. "Sugar Pie, we need to talk. Maybe at the nice little bar we used to go to. The one close to the base, remember?"

"The one you sold your drugs out of?" Amy asked dryly. "I think I'll pass."

"Oh, come on," he wheedled. "It'll be like old times."

"Leshawn, I said *no.*" Amy's voice carried across the parking lot and several in the cast turned their direction. Leshawn looked around and his eyes widened.

Good. The son of a bitch knew he had an audience.

But it didn't seem to faze him. "We need to talk," he said again. "Just you and me. Away from your sister."

"Anything you want to say to me you can say right here and right now. I don't care if Rachel hears."

His face hardened before he assumed a mask of pleasantness. "Okay, then. Amy, we belong together. You and me. We had something good going and we can have it again." He leaned forward. "It's not over between us."

"Yeah, it is." Somehow Amy managed to keep her voice level. "It's over, Leshawn. You and me. We're done. Through. Finished. Kaput."

"No, we're not." He smirked at the both of them. "We're not through. Far from it. You're gonna change your mind, Sugar Pie. You always do." He looked up over Rachel's shoulder and his smile faded entirely. "Burke," he said coldly.

"Hayes," Harlan barked in her ear.

Rachel started. She'd been so focused on Leshawn, she didn't even hear Harlan approach.

Harlan turned to Amy. "Is there a problem here?" he asked.

Amy's eyes flashed. "Mr. Hayes can't take no for an answer."

"Mr. Hayes has a problem with that," Harlan murmured.

Leshawn's eyes narrowed. "You and me got a score to settle, Burke. And we'll settle it, I promise you." He turned to Amy and his face cleared. "Now, Amy, we got no problem, because you know you don't mean it," he purred. "You think about all that sweet lovin' we used to make and see if you don't find yourself changing your mind." He winked and sauntered to a late-model Mercedes parked on the street.

"Shit, where'd he get a damned Mercedes?" Amy spat out.

"He's dealing again. Where else?" Rachel said tiredly. "Why is he so sure you'll go back to him?"

"Because I did a couple times before."

"I didn't know that. What about now?"

"No. Way. In. Hell."

"Thank you, Jesus." She turned to Harlan. "We appreciate the backup. You two have a history?"

"You might say. He tried to ream my cellmate and I beat shit out of him in the shower."

"Ewww," Rachel and Amy said in unison.

"And then he wants to screw me?" Amy added.

"Not your thing, huh?" he asked dryly. Rachel could have sworn he had a ghost of a smile on his face.

The three of them watched as Leshawn drove away. "Jesus, I wish I could do something," Amy said. "The cops don't care. Remember that clown we talked to earlier? He didn't give a shit. You know, black woman, black man, who cares?" She motioned with both hands to her face.

"You have the option of filing a stalking complaint. The cops will have to deal with him then," Rachel said.

"Like that'll stop him," Amy scoffed. "I wish I could do more than filing a damned complaint."

"So do I," Rachel added. "Don't I ever." She glanced down at her handbag.

Harlan glanced down and his eyes widened as he spotted the bulging zippers on the side of her purse. "Don't," he said sharply. "Don't even think it. You'll pay for it for the rest of your fucking life if you do."

Chapter Eleven

Rachel

Rachel and Amy got into the Charger and watched Harlan walk across the lot to his pickup. The rest of the cast drifted to their cars as well. "I guess we were the entertainment tonight," Amy murmured as Rachel pulled out of the parking lot.

"I'd rather be the evening's entertainment than the two of us having to face Leshawn by ourselves."

"How the hell did he know I was at the theater?" Amy asked.

"Any number of ways. He could've found you on the Durango Facebook page, or he could have followed us over there." An icy tendril slinked down her back and Rachel glanced over at her sister. If he was following her, Amy wasn't safe. "Right now. Get out your phone and write down everything you remember about the confrontation," Rachel said. "Word for word, as much as you can. As soon as we get home we're calling the cops. And you are filing the stalking complaint whether or not the cops think you're being stalked. That way they have to take you seriously."

"But... No, you're right. He came back around and this time he confronted me. I'll file the damned complaint, for what good it will do."

Rachel's sweaty hands gripped the wheel. They drove home in silence, Amy bent over her phone, her fingers flying. Rachel constantly looked to see if Leshawn was following them, but the Mercedes was nowhere to be seen. Nevertheless, she used the garage door opener and drove straight into the garage rather than park in the driveway as she usually did.

Once inside, they checked every door twice to make sure they were locked. Amy hit 911 while Rachel rummaged around in the refrigerator. "Damn, we're out of wine. Do I mix you a drink?"

"Did you get dispatch?"

"I did. They asked if it was an emergency and when I said no, he was gone. They said they had a lot of emergencies and they'd get here when they got here."

"Well, shit."

It was another hour before a squad car pulled up. The officer introduced himself as Officer Falkner. He was an older man who acted like he wasn't too interested until he took note of their names. He looked again at the two of them. "Your daddy a cop?" he asked curtly.

"He was," Rachel said quietly.

"Ray Castillo." They nodded and he gave them with a bittersweet smile. "Best damn cop I ever worked with." He held his pencil over his notepad. "So tell me what happened this evening. Exactly. As best you remember it."

Amy went first, using the notes she'd made on her phone. Rachel listened carefully, but Amy got it down exactly as it happened, not leaving anything out. Rachel added what little she could to Amy's account. Officer Falkner then questioned them thoroughly, making sure he had the story exactly as it happened. His eyes narrowed when Harlan's part in the confrontation came up. "How did Mr. Burke happen to be there?" he asked.

"He works at the theater," Rachel said. "He's the new set designer and tonight he was working the light board for the production."

"Either of you seeing him socially?"

Amy shook her head.

"No," Rachel said, her face flaming at the memory of their fiery kiss. "Is Harlan's being there a problem?"

"Not for your situation. But it's bad news when ex-cons hang onto their prison feuds once they're released."

"Harlan's not doing that. He's doing his damnedest to put his life back together," Rachel protested. "He's working two jobs and hasn't said or done anything to indicate otherwise."

"No desire to go back to his old life?" Falkner pressed.

"He didn't have an 'old life,'" Amy insisted. "He's the one who shot his sister's abuser."

Falkner thought a minute and nodded. His face cleared. "You're right. His situation slipped my mind for a minute. He'd be the last one to want to perpetuate a prison feud." He looked down at his notes again and shook his head. "So Hayes actually said to you you'd change your mind and come back to him because that's what you always did. Any possibility of that?"

"Nope," Amy said tightly.

"He's a cagey bastard for sure." Falkner tapped his pencil on his notepad. "He didn't overtly threaten you, which is going to make a protective order problematic. A judge is going to consider your history of taking him back. You can file a complaint for stalking."

"I will," Amy said. "He keeps threatening me. Texting. Phone messages. The note on my car. He's scaring me."

"He means to," Falkner said. "He knows exactly what he's doing. He's trying to pressure you into going back to him. And he's going about it in a way he thinks won't get him in trouble. But if you file the stalking complaint, we can pick him up and maybe get him on a parole violation and get him off the street." He smiled grimly.

"Something we would love to see," Rachel said dryly.

"Anything else I can do?" Amy asked.

"Do everything you can to build a strong case for stalking. Go back to the first time he texted you. Keep a record of all contacts. Texts, messages, phone calls, any and all confrontations. Change your phone number. Note drive-bys. If you see him again, which you shouldn't, call the police immediately. Or call me directly." He handed Amy a business card. "If I'm off duty, I'll send a cop I know who'll take you seriously. But most likely we'll pick him up and he'll be in custody."

"Thank you," Amy said.

"Anything for Ray's girls."

He gave Rachel his card and bid them a good evening. Amy shut the door behind him and sighed. "Do you think Leshawn will really go back to jail?"

"Wouldn't bet my next paycheck on it," Rachel stated. "At least Officer Falkner takes us seriously. The first cop sure as hell didn't."

Amy rolled her eyes. "The only reason this cop gave a damn is because of Daddy. If we weren't Ray's girls, do you think this guy would've cared?"

"I hope so, but probably not. It shouldn't make a difference who we are or who our father was. They ought to give a damn about every woman who calls, not only the daughters of an old friend. It frustrates the hell out of me."

"Makes me understand Harlan a little better," Amy mused. "Especially if the man beat the shit out of his sister. He shouldn't have done it, but—" She shrugged.

"Yeah, but. I guess I can understand him a little too, but I'll never be convinced he had to go as far as committing murder," Rachel said knowing she'd looked down at her concealed-carry bag thinking like Dirty Harry.

***

Rachel stood at the door of the women's dressing room and laughed. "Letti, if the wig and the makeup are as good as the costume, you're gonna be the best Grandma Addams ever. Quite properly evil."

Letti looked at herself in the mirror and made a face. "Everly doesn't think I need the wig and makeup. She thinks I'm evil already. The little toot got mad at Mommy today."

"What did Mommy do to make her mad?" Amy asked.

"Mommy fussed at her for running out in the street. She does not like to be fussed at."

"Aww, poor baby. Does Daddy fuss at her, too?" Rachel asked.

Letti rolled her eyes. "Do you think he'd fuss at her? He tries to reason with her like she's ten and not two. Makes me crazy."

"He needs to get a handle on being firm with her or he's gonna have trouble on his hands when she's a tweenie," Sasha said. "My brother made that mistake and lived to regret it."

They all looked at Sasha in surprise. It was the first time she'd contributed to a conversation that wasn't theater related.

"You are so right," Letti said. "He needs to be firm. Maybe you could say something to that effect in front of Kevin sometime. I can't get through to him."

"Uh, sure." They waited for her to say more but she folded back into herself.

Rachel turned to Amy. "If your costume was any tighter you couldn't breathe."

"I can't breathe now. I don't know if I can dance in this thing." She danced a few steps and shook her head. "It's gonna make it hard. They're going to have to let the seams out."

"Ladies, we need to get seated so I can go over some things." Rachel said.

The women trooped down the side stairs and sat in the first row. Rachel spotted Noel and Harlan at their respective boards and motioned for them to come down front. They sat together on the second row next to some of the women in the ensemble.

Damn if he didn't look good. Healthier, and happier. She felt guilty she'd caused a cloud to hang over his head while he was doing such great work for the theater. And her stomach knotting up every time she saw him didn't say she was forgetting how she felt about him. Especially now. Because of the mess with Leshawn, she was beginning to understand the emotions that'd driven Harlan to do what he did.

She didn't agree with it and never would, but she was beginning to feel his frustration and fear for his sister. Rachel was feeling the same for Amy.

Rachel shared a few more suggestions she'd thought of during the day. "Before we go through the play again, I need to see Morticia and Gomez's tango in costume."

Amy and Eric went up on stage. Amy was forced to hike up the skirt to climb the steps. "How much of it do you want us to do?" she asked.

"Enough to see if the skirt's a problem."

It was. They were barely three bars in before it was obvious the skirt was seriously hampering Amy's movement. Rachel called a halt and motioned them to stop. "I need to see the dress up close. The rest of you, we start in fifteen minutes. Take your places and Miranda will call time." She turned to Amy. "Let me see."

Rachel bent down and looked at the left side seam and then flipped it so she could see inside. To her immense relief, there was plenty of fabric on either side of the stitching. "I'll call the costumer in the morning. She'll have to let it out. Sasha's too. You need room to move."

"What about the damned bodice? I'm suffocating here," Amy groused.

She grinned at Amy. "The top is fine. You don't need to breathe...much."

"Yeah, right. Between this damn costume and Leshawn I might not breathe for the next six months."

"Is this the same Leshawn you were yelling at in the parking lot last night?" Letti asked.

"Yeah. Such a charming way to end the evening." Amy's lips tightened. "A fight with my asshole ex and some quality time with SAPD."

"So, what was the upshot?" Harlan asked.

"About what you'd expect." Amy made a face. "We called the police when we got home, and it took an hour before one showed. I filed a stalking complaint. Supposedly they'll jail him for a parole violation. But they have to find him first to pick him up."

Harlan snorted. "They're not going to go out of their way to find him. They don't give a damn."

"Actually, this cop does. He's an old friend of Daddy's," Rachel said then frowned. "Though, he still didn't offer us much by way of hope this would end right away."

"Sucks," Letti said.

"Totally. I wish there was more we could do." Rachel shook her head.

"I don't know what that would be, since you're not inclined to take my route," Harlan stated.

Rachel winced and Letti's eyes widened.

"No, she isn't," Amy snapped. "And neither am I." She turned to Rachel. "I'll rehearse in something else." She jerked up her skirt and flounced up the stairs.

Harlan made a face as she stomped out of sight. "I didn't mean to upset her."

"She didn't get much sleep last night. Neither did I," Rachel said. "She's tired and on edge and she feels bad about worrying me," Rachel said quietly. "She feels like her shit is flowing into my life." Enough of this. Rachel looked at her watch. "Ten minutes, folks. We have a play to rehearse."

Chapter Twelve

Harlan

Harlan stood tensely at the back of the theater. He wiped his sweaty hands on his jeans and for the twentieth time adjusted the microphone in his ear. "I give all my directions verbally. You'll want to listen for when I cue you on the lights," Miranda explained.

"You? Not Rachel?"

Miranda laughed. "I see no one has explained my role to you. Rachel's last night of responsibility will be Thursday at the dress rehearsal. Then she bows out and pats herself on the back for a job well done and I take over. I manage the live productions. I call time and give all the instructions. I'll be the one leading the post-mortems, not her."

"Okay. I learn something new every day, and this was mine for today," he said.

"Ten minutes," she told him.

He perched on his stool and tried to calm his pounding heart as his gaze roamed the set. Everyone said it looked great. He took pride in designing and building it, and learning he could do the lights confirmed Josh hadn't been wrong to put his faith in him.

The extra money from the lighting job was a welcome boost. He needed tuition money and was seriously jonesing to replace his old truck, which had developed a suspicious ping when he accelerated. He might be able to find another used truck, but in better shape than the ancient Chevy. Something with an air-conditioned cab and nice enough to take a woman out on a date. *She's not going to want to go out in a pickup. Not when she drives a brand-new Charger.*

He shut down that train of thought, only to have the object of his dreams walk in with of a couple in their late middle-age, and two of the cutest grandmas he'd seen in a long time. The one who had to be Granny was a tiny, birdlike woman, with bright eyes shining out of a wrinkled, smiling face. *Abuela* was plump and even at her advanced age was almost as tall as Rachel. She wore a blasé expression he'd bet was entirely for show.

Rachel's mother was on the arm of a distinguished looking man, and was as gorgeous as her daughters. Harlan could understand how Ray Castillo had fallen under her spell. Rachel ushered them down almost all the way to the front and made sure they were seated before coming up the aisle. Her expression was tense and he could understand why. *The Addams Family* was her baby and as of tonight she was handing it over to a cast and crew who would do a fine job, him included.

Miranda called the five-minute mark. Josh and Cameron hustled in with a couple of tweens and sat in the back row. Harlan looked at the kids wistfully. He'd missed those years with Nathan and Evie, and now they didn't have much interest in reconnecting with him.

They didn't act like they were angry with him for killing their father. No doubt, Carrie had explained he'd saved her life and probably theirs as well. But at their age, they had their friends and activities, and had no desire to get to know him.

They hadn't even wanted to come tonight. He'd invited them and Carrie yesterday afternoon at Thanksgiving dinner, but Carrie had to work and the kids had already made plans with their friends. Like so many of his jailhouse dreams, a close relationship with his niece and nephew didn't look like it would ever come to pass.

Miranda came over and sat on a tall stool on the other side of Noah, from which she would supervise most of the production. "Lower house lights," she murmured to him through the mic. "Spotlight on Rachel."

Harlan lowered the house lights. Rachel strode down the aisle and climbed the center steps to the stage. Gradually, he eased the switch to the on position and she was bathed in the spotlight. If she was still tense, it didn't show. She radiated welcoming confidence shining out from her expression and body language. She welcomed everyone with warmth and sincerity, making special mention of the children in the audience, and reminded the patrons of the homeless shelter the theater was sponsoring this Christmas. Then she spread her arms wide and with a huge smile on her face said, "Now the Durango Street Theatre presents *The Addams Family.*"

She hopped down off the stage and Miranda cued the orchestra. The prelude began and he dimmed the stage lights, giving the ensemble time to hit their marks in front of the gravestones. As the orchestra played its last notes, Miranda cued him and slowly, he illuminated the stage.

Morticia, Gomez and the ensemble were ready for their spooky dance in the Addams graveyard.

The show was on.

It didn't take him long to relax and get into the groove, along with everyone else. The singing, dancing, and acting was superb. He'd been impressed with the cast during rehearsals, but tonight they came alive in a new way.

Sasha was flawless as the daughter of the wacky family, and Kevin as her clueless boyfriend. The actors playing Pugsley and Fester and the Beinekes were spot-on. Letti was almost but not quite stealing the show as Grandma Addams, spooky and weird and funny all at the same time. Eric was a laughable, believable Gomez.

But the one who was knocking it out of the ballpark was Amy. She was absolutely perfect as the strange, sexy, kooky matriarch of this dysfunctional clan. Hilarious and poignant, she managed to nail the character of Morticia, who was feeling older and less relevant to her family in the face of her daughter's engagement to a *normal* young man. She played the role with the perfect combination of comedy and pathos, making Morticia funny and sympathetic at the same time.

As he lowered the lights for a scene change, he wondered how much of tonight's excellence was due to the actors' talent, and how much was due to Rachel's direction.

The first act passed quickly. Miranda cued the house lights and the audience streamed to the lobby restrooms and to the snack bar. Rachel's family joined the exodus, but Rachel wasn't with them. He wondered briefly where she went and if Leshawn had come back around. But he'd be damned if he brought it up.

He made a much-needed pit stop, and as he was stepping out of the restroom he spotted Rachel across the lobby talking with a couple of men, one of whom was to die for handsome and the other would've been but for the scarring on his face.

Harlan's groin tightened as he was flooded with an angry jolt on adrenaline he recognized as jealousy. He watched with hooded eyes as she laughed at something one of them said, and when the younger, handsome one gave her a tight hug and a kiss on the cheek it was all he could do not to cross the lobby and yank her out of his arms.

He had no claim on her, yet she was *his*. He stomped back to the light board and resumed his post. While Rachel had told him she wasn't interested, she'd never said she wasn't attracted to him—and he knew she was. On more than one occasion, he'd caught her glancing at him with an expression filled with longing. If anyone knew how precious time was and not to waste it, Harlan did. Stupid to have so much chemistry and let it go to waste when no one was promised tomorrow.

Unfortunately, there was no convincing her otherwise.

Miranda sat on her stool and cued him to blink the house lights. It took only minutes for the lingerers to scurry back to their seats before she cued the lights to go down and the orchestra to begin the prelude to the second act. As he slowly lowered the lights, he saw Rachel slip in, but rather than sit near the front with her family, she slid into a chair on the side aisle of the back row. She looked around and caught Miranda's eye and sent her a visual signal of some kind. Miranda nodded and jotted something down on her note pad.

Hmm. Harlan's lips twitched. It didn't look like she'd turned over the reins completely. At least not yet.

The second act went as smoothly as the first. He caught a glitch or two, but they weren't anything the audience would notice, and he'd bet his old pickup Miranda would have it straightened out by the next performance.

The production proceeded to its inevitable, hilarious conclusion, and the orchestra played as the cast came out to take their bows. He wasn't surprised when both Letti and Amy got standing ovations.

The actors paraded up the side aisles and lined up across the lobby. He turned on the house lights and the audience flocked to the lobby as well. Noah shut down the sound board and took off his mic. "Is there anything you need to take up with me before I go?" he asked Miranda. "I really need to get out of here."

"You're not going down to Thirties and throw back a few? You usually do on opening night," Miranda teased.

"Naw. Jeannie's pregnant and feels like shit and I told her I'd bring her a carton of Rocky Road. Which is why I'd like to leave now if I could. I'm worried about her."

"Hey, congratulations," Harlan said even as a pang of envy shot through him. If things had been different, he might have been married with a family by now.

Miranda looked down her notes. "Act two, scene two. You were a tad slow getting Amy's mic back on. You need to have it on by the time the lights come up. Otherwise, I didn't catch anything. Tell Jeannie to hang in there, it doesn't last forever. In a few months she'll feel fine." She winked.

"How encouraging," Noah said dryly. "Thanks for letting me go."

"You going to Thirties?" Harlan asked Miranda.

She laughed. "Me? No. My sweetie and I are both recovering alcoholics. It's the last place we belong."

"Ain't it the truth?" A tall, thin man with a weathered face put his arm around her and kissed her cheek. "As soon as she's set the cast and crew on the straight and narrow, we'll be hitting the hamburger joint on the way out of town for burgers and shakes."

"You two haven't met. Ross, this is Harlan. He's our new set designer and light man."

The man immediately offered his hand. "Ross Ellis. Glad to meet you. Love the set." He turned to Miranda. "I'll meet you in the parking lot when you're done. I've gotta go bug Kevin." His eyes danced wickedly.

Miranda laughed. "Kevin will love that. Long story," she added when Harlan looked puzzled. "What about you? Are you headed to the local watering hole?"

"Nah. I doubt they'd want my company. I wouldn't feel comfortable anyway. I don't have any friends in the Durango crowd."

Miranda shrugged. "I think you're wrong about them not wanting your company, and the only way you're going to make friends and feel comfortable is to get to know them. But I'm a great one to talk. I'm not going, either. You may as well shut down the light board and get a soda. I have a lot to get through, and unlike Noah, you don't have an excuse to leave early."

He shut down the board and wandered out to the lobby. The cast was greeting their enthusiastic audience and accepting their well-earned accolades. He got a soda and a piece of opening-night cake and took it back to the auditorium where he sat in the front and waited for the cast and crew to assemble for Miranda's post-mortem.

The crew scuttled around the stage, readying it for tomorrow night. The cast wandered in one at a time. Josh and Cameron were nowhere to be seen, but Rachel sat to the side of the row. Miranda stood in front of them and the crew stopped what they were doing and joined them in the front of the auditorium. She consulted her notes and addressed her concerns one at a time, touching on each briefly with confidence the issue would be resolved by the next performance.

The crew returned to the stage, and the cast headed for the parking lot. He noticed the two guys who'd been talking to Rachel earlier were in the parking lot as well, seemingly waiting for someone. Rachel? His teeth ground together and he reminded himself she didn't want him and it was none of his business. He was about to get in his truck and go back to his place when Letti and her young husband caught up to him. "You coming to thirties?" Kevin asked.

"No. I think I'll head back to my place."

"Aw, come on. We all need to celebrate. We did a bang-up job tonight, and a big part of it was your spectacular sets," Kevin wheedled.

Harlan hesitated, tempted. It might be fun. But then he spotted Rachel and Amy coming out of the theater and shook his head. "I don't think so. There are those who would have more fun if I weren't there."

Letti glanced over at Rachel and Amy and raised her eyebrow. "There are those who might benefit from getting to know you better." She motioned to Rachel and Amy. "I'm having a hard time convincing Harlan to come with us tonight. You two want to put your two cents in?"

Harlan's face flamed. Amy smiled and nodded as she approached them. "Come on. You've worked long and hard on this production, as long and hard as anybody. You deserve to celebrate its success with us."

"You do," Rachel said, her voice and her smile sincere. "Besides, their parking lot's most likely full and we're going to have to walk, and I wouldn't mind having you walk with us like you did the night of Miguel's party."

Harlan nodded. "Okay. I'll come. Thanks for including me." He wasn't convinced it was the best idea in the world, but it was the first time Rachel had reached out to him, and he'd be damned if he'd throw it back in her face.

Even if she was sweet on the good-looking guy.

Letti and Kevin opted to walk too. He maneuvered to walk between Rachel and Amy, with a lady on either side of him. This was the closest he'd been to Rachel since their scorching kiss a month ago. He was close enough to catch the occasional whiff of her perfume and feel the warmth of her body close to his triggering the desire he felt during their embrace and the urge to take her into his arms again. Her smile was big and her stride confident, like she didn't have a care in the world. But more than once he caught Amy looking around, checking the street and glancing down the darkened alleyways. He tried not to react to the memories of Carrie doing the same damn thing the last two years of Abernathy's life. He wouldn't let the old ghosts make him cross and irritable. They'd paid him the compliment of inviting him to their celebration. The last thing he wanted to do was let his ill temper spoil it for the Castillo sisters or anyone else.

The bar was crowded, but Letti and Kevin pointed to a large alcove in the back with familiar faces at some of the tables. With them in the lead, the group weaved their way through the crowded room to where Eric and some of the cast were holding tables. Letti spotted Rachel's good-looking guy and his friend sitting with the couple playing the Beinekes. They were holding a big table along the wall and motioned for them to come. Rachel and Amy smiled and headed straight for their table.

Of course, Rachel would want to sit with her sweetie.

But maybe he wasn't.

Letti and Amy collected the same hugs and kisses Rachel had, and the men greeted Kevin with bro-hugs. Letti sat down beside the scarred guy and immediately began a conversation about Sophie and tuition. When he spotted the men's matching wedding rings and noticed them holding hands under the table, his first reaction was a surprised *How about that* and his second was one of immense, ridiculous relief.

The hot stud wasn't Rachel's boyfriend.

The hot stud was married to Letti's ex.

The world sure had changed while he was locked away.

Rachel introduced him to Letti's ex, Owen. The stud muffin was Wade. John and Celia Marsh, the actors playing the Beinekes, introduced themselves as well. He sat down between Rachel and Kevin with Amy and the Marshes on the end. The server took their orders for drinks and three big platters of bar food.

Talk was of tonight's success and conversation flowed freely, particularly after the interesting assortment of drinks was delivered. Harlan gathered from the lively exchanges that they all had been friends for years and shared quite a bit of history at the Durango. Owen and Wade, and Letti and Kevin had met through the theater, and Owen and Letti had done shows together while they were married. It made him wonder if Rachel met the men she dated there as well. It would make sense if she did.

Maybe Amy should start selecting her boyfriends from the men at the Durango. They'd be a whole lot better choice than Leshawn Hayes.

The table got quiet for a few minutes when three heaping platters of buffalo wings, quesadillas, mini tacos, fried mozzarella sticks, and jalapeno poppers were delivered. Dinner had been sketchy, if they had eaten anything at all, and every one of them was starving. They stripped the platters clean and placed an order for a fourth platter and another round of drinks, which they finished as well.

Finally, they began to push their plates away, and Wade said, "An excellent end to an excellent day." "Here's hoping the rest of the performances go as smoothly."

There was a round of *Here, here*, and *We hope*. Harlan looked around. "Does a smooth opening night mean you can expect problems later on?"

The rest of the table looked at one another. "Not usually," Letti said. "It normally means the opposite."

"Not always," Owen and Wade said in unison.

"*How to Succeed in Business*," Wade added.

"Oh, that's right. I'd forgotten," Rachel said. "It ended up turning out so well."

"What happened?" Harlan asked.

"I don't know this story either," Kevin said.

"I was playing the lead and had a burst appendix during the second week of production. Owen stepped in for the rest of the run," Wade said. "He did a bang-up job." He looked at Owen with love shining from his eyes. "It got him back on the stage and me the love of my life."

"It got me the love of my life too, along with the miracle makeup that can make these," Owen gestured to his mangled face, "temporarily go away.".

"Best story ever," Rachel said. "Except for maybe theirs." She pointed to Letti and Kevin. "She passed out in front of our biggest donors."

"And went home to the best news we could imagine," Kevin added. "She was pregnant with Everly."

Amy looked from Wade to Letti and laughed. "Tell you what. Neither of those scenarios especially appeals to me. Y'all can keep your best stories ever awards." Her smile faded. "I don't want any more drama surrounding *Addams Family*. I had enough the other night."

Letti asked, "Has he been back?"

"No. At least not yet." Amy's smile vanished entirely. "I'm not convinced he got the message. He didn't act like it the other night."

"It's time you called the police," Owen said,

"You really should," Wade added. "Bastard's getting away with stalking you."

"Ya think?" Amy asked sarcastically. "The cops have been out twice. The first cop could've cared less. The second one told me to file a stalking complaint. Which I did. He said they'd pick him up and it'll probably be a parole violation, but he's hiding from them."

"They won't do anything if they find him," Harlan said before he could stop himself. "They're not gonna do a damn thing to stop him,.

She can call until she's blue in the face and file all the stalking complaints she wants. God knows I called them often enough. It didn't do a damn bit of good then and it won't now."

"It didn't do any good because your sister wouldn't take the steps she needed to in order to stop him," Owen said.

"What...do you mean by that?" Harlan sputtered. "They knew what was going on. They didn't care."

"Like hell," Owen shot back. "Harlan, we cared a lot. We answered those calls. Over and over. I caught two of them myself. Every one of us at the northwest substation knew who Carrie Burke and Cole Abernathy were. We knew who you were, and what was going on. But we couldn't deal with it as it needed to be dealt with because your sister wouldn't cooperate."

"That's ridiculous. I called and called over and over. I begged you to do something."

"You're right. *You* called. *You* filed the complaint. *You* begged. So we went. We arrested him more than once, and even got him incarcerated for a little while. But she refused to support us. She'd make excuses, and the second time we arrested him she refused to testify."

"Of course she did. She was terrified of him. Afraid he'd take her kids away from her. With his parents' money, he could have. Hell, the one time it did get as far as a trial, the fancy-assed lawyer his daddy paid for got him off with a slap on the wrist. He whipped up on her the minute he got out of jail, and she wouldn't testify the second time because he threatened her with more than taking away the kids. At that point he disappeared for long enough for Carrie to let her guard down, which is when he came back and beat hell out of her." Harlan's lips twisted bitterly.

"I know. It drove us nuts. But the law is the law, and sometimes the laws tie our hands. You have no idea how deeply the case affected us, especially after you blew him away because we'd done all we could. The cops who had to arrest you were not happy about doing it. They regretted having to take you in, and they hated they were rendered powerless."

Harlan blinked. They cared about Carrie? They felt bad about having to arrest him? He had no idea.

And he didn't have an answer for Owen.

Not that Owen gave him a chance to. He turned to Amy. "Did either of the officers you talked with explain what you should do and what to expect?"

"Officer Falkner did. He's an old friend of Daddy's."

"Horace Falkner? He's a good cop. So I don't have to go over it with you."

"No, I've taken the steps he recommended. I won't be making any excuses for Leshawn, I promise you. I filed the charges so they can arrest him, put him back in jail, and get him away from me. But will they do it? Will it take him doing what he's doing twenty times before he's arrested? It's like the cops won't really care until I get hurt."

Owen's jaw muscles jumped. "It doesn't take twenty times, and you don't have to get hurt. Sounds like you've done what you need to do. If nothing happens, you let me know."

Amy nodded and Rachel's mouth was tight, but she nodded too.

After a few awkward moments of silence, Letti asked Owen and Wade when they planned to do another show and Rachel told them about securing an upcoming production of *Kinky Boots*.

Harlan sat quietly while the conversation flowed around him. He couldn't get Owen's comments out of his brain. After all these years, hearing the story from a law officer's point of view, he realized Carrie had needed to do more. But his sister was paralyzed with fear, beaten down from years with the SOB, and convinced he would take her children if she tried to fight back. Knowing Abernathy, he would've tried. But Harlan had no idea the police gave a damn about what was going on. He thought they didn't care.

According to Owen, they did. They cared a lot.

Which was a stunner for him.

They all finished their drinks. Letti and Kevin excused themselves, saying they needed to relieve the babysitter. Amy stood too and looked at Rachel. "I hate to be a party pooper, but I'm fried. Do you mind if we go?"

"Don't mind at all." But she looked disappointed and he could sympathize. Aside from the ugly trip down memory lane and Amy's stalker, Rachel seemed to be enjoying the evening as was he.

Before his brain engaged, his mouth was moving. "If you want to send Amy home in the car, I don't mind getting you home later." Stupid, stupid, stupid. She wouldn't want him to drive her home.

Then she surprised him when she nodded and said, "Okay." She snapped the car key from her keychain and handed it to Amy. "Be careful. I've only made a few payments."

Amy grinned and left with Letti and Kevin.

Everyone left at the table ordered dessert and another round of drinks, mostly nonalcoholic, and started talking about more juicy Durango gossip, of which there seemed to be an unending supply.

It was another hour before they were ready to call it quits. His truck was still in the theater parking lot. The other two couples were parked across the street from the bar and said their good nights at the front door. He offered Rachel his arm. She took it without hesitation and they started down the deserted sidewalk not saying anything for most of the first block.

"Did you have fun?" she asked as they stopped at the corner.

"I did. Thanks for the encouragement. I would've gone home otherwise."

"I'm glad you came."

They crossed the street and walked on. The air was cool and the night quiet. The moon had set while they were in Thirties, and a handful of stars could be seen in the light-polluted sky.

Her hand was firm on his arm and he could feel the warmth of her body as they walked in the peaceful darkness. The scent of her perfume teased him as they approached the theater parking lot. He'd never been so aware of a woman in his life.

A woman who didn't want him, he reminded himself.

A woman who wouldn't look beyond his past to the man behind it.

A woman who'd turned him away.

Yet, he still lusted after her.

They got to the theater's lot and he gestured to his truck, parked under a streetlight. "My chariot," he said ruefully. "I hope to get a better one soon."

"It's fine."

He heard her breath hitch and turned to find her staring at him with the same lust he was feeling for her. "Don't." He said low. "Don't look at me like you want to kiss me."

"But, damn it, I do want to kiss you."

"No, you don't. Get in the damned truck."

She didn't listen and grabbed the sides of his face and pulled him close. He thought to pull away, but the yearning he'd been trying to ignore was too strong.

He bent forward and touched her lips in a hard and hungry kiss.

He wrapped his arms around her waist and yanked her close until they were plastered together from chest to thigh. His tongue demanded entrance to her sweetness, and she complied. She tasted of hot sauce, Moscato, and sweet, warm, willing woman.

The woman who starred in his dreams for too long.

The woman he wanted in his bed.

Her body told him, she wanted him just as much.

Her arms enveloped him and her hard nipples dug into his chest as she ran her fingers up and down his back, pulling him closer than he thought possible.

His rock-hard cock nestled between the inviting vee at the top of her thighs, promising everything he wanted. Holding her was better than the best fantasy he could come up with.

He longed to lay her down, strip her naked, and do all sorts of wicked things to her. He desperately wanted to explore her beautiful body and make her scream with pleasure as she came for him over and over.

Maybe he would get that chance, or maybe this kiss was as good as it got.

If this was all she would give him, he'd make it a kiss they'd remember for all time.

They clung to each other for long minutes, kissing, touching, and caressing until she her hold loosened. He lifted his head and pulled away slightly.

"Enough to hold you for the next month, or would you like more?" he asked quietly.

She stared at him a bit dazed. "I've wanted to kiss you again immediately after you kissed me the last time."

"Not what I asked. I asked if you wanted more. Or is this kiss another one and done?"

"What exactly are you asking me?"

"Do I put you in the truck and take you home, or do we walk down to the little motel on the next block and finish what we started? Your decision." He looked into her eyes. "Do you want me, knowing who I am and what I did, or are we back to where we've been before?"

His hopes crashed as she opened the passenger door. A kiss like she'd laid on him and she was still going to turn him down.

Then she turned back to look at him with a crooked smile. "The place down the street's a dump. There's a much nicer one on Austin Highway a few blocks from the house for about the same price. I'll give you directions."

He moved fast and planted a hard, sweet kiss on her lips. "Show me the way."

Chapter Thirteen

Rachel

She was certifiably crazy. *Loco.* Out of her mind.

But she was still going to a hotel room with Harlan.

He pulled into the parking lot then asked, "You know this place?" In the winking light of the vintage neon sign she could see the ghost of a smile on his lips.

"Not personally. Amy's mentioned it once or twice. She came here with another one of her losers."

"Leshawn's not the only one?"

"You don't want to know."

He hopped out and circled the truck to open the door for her. He took her hand and together they jogged to the office where a sleepy-looking clerk watched something on his iPad. Harlan asked the price and whipped out his wallet, counting out the cash. The clerk handed over a keycard. "Room one-thirty-two. It's out back and there's a designated parking space."

Harlan moved the truck to the marked space. It took him two tries swiping the key card before the door would open. They barely got inside before they were wrapped in one another's arms, kissing each other with a month's worth of pent-up hunger. His hands were all over her as he caressed her back and then lowered them to cup her butt. His cock swelled against the vee between her legs and she felt herself begin to dampen.

"I've dreamed about this for the last month. No, longer," he murmured against her lips. "I've wanted you since the first time I laid eyes on you. I've wanted you every time I've seen you."

"I've wanted you too," she said.

"Let's do something about it." He took a step back and shucked the long-sleeved shirt he'd worn as a jacket. Beneath it an *Addams Family* t-shirt stretched across his broad shoulders.

That went next, leaving him bare to the waist. Rachel gulped and stared.

His chest was as pale as his face had been and was covered with a thick tangle of dark hair that arrowed down to a narrow band disappearing into his jeans. Muscles rippled under the skin of his chest and shoulders, and his arms were thickly corded. She reached out and dug her fingers into the mat on his chest. "Nice," she breathed.

He took her face in his hands and placed the gentlest of kisses on her lips. "Want to take some of those clothes off?"

She nodded and slipped off her cardigan. Her knit top followed leaving her clad in a lace-trimmed black bra. She looked down and made a face. "If I'd known I would have worn something prettier than this."

Harlan reached behind her and unhooked the bra. Before she could object he tossed it on the carpet beside the bed and gazed down at it. "It looks perfectly beautiful to me," he said low.

She smiled. "You have a point."

His lust-laden stare ate up her chocolate-tipped breasts. "Here's what's beautiful." He touched a swollen nipple with his fingertip.

She swallowed as a shiver went down her back. She stepped out of her shoes, and her skinny pants were next, leaving her in a pair of high cut panties that weren't the sexiest in the world but weren't too bad.

Never taking his gaze off her, Harlan sat on the bed, kicked off his shoes, and shrugged out of his jeans and boxer briefs in one motion.

Her eyes widened at the sight of his swollen cock, thrusting up from another lush nest of tangled brown hair. "Not a bit shy, are you?"

He gestured to her underwear. "Time for you not to be either. Or are you waiting for me to help you?"

He hooked his thumbs in the sides of her panties and pulled them down her legs. "Jesus, you're gorgeous," he breathed as he stared at her naked body. He reached around and pulled her on top of him. "That's better. Much, much better," he said as he rolled her on her back and scooted beside her. "Ready?"

She nodded and then they were all over each other, kissing and touching and caressing anywhere and everywhere they could reach. His lips were on her breasts, her hands were on his cock, his fingers were on his waist, her lips were trailing down his abdomen.

She held nothing back. She had no idea where this might take them and right now she didn't care. She was in his arms and he was in hers and nothing else mattered.

His lips curled around her nipple and his tongue rasped the knotted tip. He paid homage to her other nipple before trailing down her body to just above her core. He paid attention to each part of her body with care, but at the same time there was urgency in to his touch fueld by a deep hunger.

Harlan motioned for her to part her legs as his lips trailed down and he was right there. His mouth over her core. She froze momentarily—most of her lovers hadn't liked this much—but she let her legs fall apart.

He pushed them even wider and then he feasted, first with tender but sensual attention from his fingers and then with a breathtaking erotic assault by his lips and tongue. Rachel's heart pounded against her ribs, and her breathing grew ragged. The things he was doing to her... No lover had ever aroused her body or her emotions like he did.

She gasped and thrashed as the tension grew, slowly at first, and then in an erotic spiral spinning higher and higher until her entire body exploded in shuddering waves. Hard contractions shook her from her hair to her toes as she came in an orgasm like no other she'd ever experienced.

She collapsed onto the bed, convinced the best was over.

But Harlan had other ideas.

He gave her a moment and then resumed the sensual assault, and to her amazement Rachel felt herself spiraling out of control yet again, tumbling for a second time into an explosion of ecstasy. He took her with his lips yet a third time, waiting for the spasms to subside before raising his body and moving his big frame between her legs.

Somehow, somewhere he'd found a condom and put it on, and then he slid into her wet, slick body.

"Heaven," he breathed. "The closest I've been to Heaven in a damned long time."

He gave her body time to acclimate before he began to move inside her, slowly at first and then faster. She'd thought after three earth-shaking orgasms she was spent. But incredibly, she felt herself rising again, this time in unison with him. When he must've felt her stiffen and pulse around him in an unbelievable fourth orgasm, he went off with her, the two of them crying out as they came apart in one another's arms. His orgasm seemed to go on forever, as his body shook and trembled above her.

When his shuddering subsided, he rolled them to their sides, careful not to break their connection. He looked into her eyes and his brow dropped. "You feel...okay?"

Rachel looked at him disbelievingly. "You can't tell? Best I've had in maybe forever. Why?"

He looked at her and she'd never seen anyone turn so red. "I wasn't sure. It's been years since I've been with a woman. I wasn't the most experienced man out there before, you know." He withdrew from her body, and she missed him. He disappeared into the bathroom, reappearing without the condom. He got back in bed and lay down beside her. "I missed out on the experience most men get in their twenties." He stared up at the ceiling. "Like everything else I should've been doing in my twenties."

She snuggled against him. "I promise you. I've never had four orgasms with anybody."

"I don't have to worry, then."

"No, you don't have a thing to worry about." She felt his cock start to swell against her thigh. "Except if you don't have any more condoms."

"One more. I thought carrying any more with me was being unreasonably optimistic."

She grinned. He was sweet. She found his uncertainty endearing at the same time her heart hurt for all he'd lost. An emotion she didn't expect given her unassailable conviction he'd been where he belonged.

"Let's put it to good use, and then we can do some of the other stuff you might have missed out on over the years."

Harlan laughed. "Sounds good."

He reached for his wallet and withdrew another condom. This time their lovemaking was slower and the sense of urgency had abated.

They gave themselves over to the pure enjoyment of one another, of tasting and touching each other with bold abandon. They held nothing back. Rachel marveled at the wonder, the pleasure, the delight of being in his arms. He brought her to two more shattering climaxes with his lips before entering her a second time. They soared to the pinnacle together again, crying out and gasping one another's name as they came apart in each other's arms.

He eased away from her momentarily and disposed of the condom. "Crap, it's late," he said as he looked at his phone. "Do I need to set the alarm?"

"Not really. We're having lunch with Mom and Harold and the grandmas, but not until one or so. I doubt Amy expects me."

Harlan's face furrowed. "She's going to wonder."

Rachel threw her arm across his chest. "No, she's not. She knows we have the hots for each other."

"Okay." He kissed her temple and settled her head on his shoulder. "'Night."

"'Night."

He dropped off immediately and she wasn't long after. She slept hard and dreamlessly, curled up next to Harlan's warm, hard body, and pushed his hand away when he ran it down the side of her face. "Let me sleep."

Harlan laughed. "Wake up, sleepyhead. Or are you planning to sleep away the entire day?"

"Sounds good," she mumbled into his chest. "What time is it?"

"Nine-thirty. You must've been tired."

"I was. You must have been as tired. Unless you've been awake for a while?"

"No. Ten minutes, maybe. You're beautiful when you're asleep."

"You're sexy as hell when you lie."

"What makes you think I'm lying?" He planted a tender kiss on her lips and she felt his cock start to swell next to her leg. "Shit. I should have brought more condoms."

Rachel reached down and felt his cock. "Or we can do some of those things you missed out on in your twenties. Things not requiring a condom." She raised a brow as she grasped his cock and pumped up and down.

"Uh, feels...sounds good to me."

She grinned wickedly as she scooted into position. Her lips surrounded the tip and she sucked lightly for a moment before taking him fully into her mouth, pushing him back onto the bed when he tried to sit up. It didn't take her long to have him writhing and moaning. She doubled her efforts and was rewarded as he stiffened beneath her and jetted into the back of her throat with a deep guttural groan.

Never quite sure what to do with a mouthful of come, she bolted for the bathroom and spit it into the sink, accompanied by his deep laughter. She glared at him as she stomped back to the bed. "I don't do that with everyone," she announced loftily.

"Then I'm doubly honored." He pushed her down in the covers. "Let me see if I can return the favor."

He put what he'd learned about her responsiveness to good use, and it wasn't long before she was enjoying yet another orgasm, courtesy of his lips and tongue. They cuddled together for a bit and then she sat up. "I better shower and get on back. As much as I'd like to spend the day here with you."

"Your lunch date," he said. "You want to go first, or shall I?" He grinned. "I'd suggest we shower together, but we'd never get you home on time."

"I'll go. It will take me longer to put myself back together afterwards."

He shook his head. "You don't need to put yourself together. You look great exactly the way God made you."

"Thanks." She smiled shyly and ducked into the bathroom.

She made quick work of the shower. By the time she was finished, he'd gathered up her clothes and piled them on the bathroom counter. She dressed quickly and returned to the room, where he lounged on the bed in all his naked glory. And what a sight he was. His chiseled body a delicious sight in the light of day. It was all she could do not to strip off and go another round with him. Instead, she pointed her thumb in the direction of the bathroom. "Your turn."

By the time he was finished, she'd used a pick on her damp curls and added the lip gloss and mascara she carried with her. He pulled on his clothes and sat on the side of the bed to put on his shoes. "Looking forward to lunch with your family?"

"Honestly? No. We haven't told Mom and Harold about the shit with Leshawn yet. The grandmas don't know either. I dread the round of *tut-tuts* and *I told you so's* Amy's gonna get."

"Why would they tell her that? She's trying to do something about him."

"Because we all tried to tell her from the get-go he was bad news and she wouldn't listen. Mom is particularly unsympathetic. She has excellent taste in men and expected her daughters to have the same. Amy has disappointed her."

He made a face. "She wouldn't be too enamored of your current choice, either."

"Probably not. But the situation's different. You were trying to protect a foolish woman. You weren't the one who created the problem. Your sister was."

Harlan's eyes narrowed. "'Foolish' is a harsh word for a woman you've never met."

Rachel threw the pick back in her purse. "You're right. I haven't. I'm basing my opinion on what Owen said last night. He laid it out. She wouldn't testify against him."

"She was afraid," Harlan stated. "Beat down and terrified. Abernathy told her if she testified against him, he'd go to court and take the kids away. Knowing him, he would've done it. Or at least tried. His parents were loaded and could've paid for a legal fight. Carrie could protect them if they were with her. She couldn't protect them if he got them. She did what she felt she had to do."

"She couldn't testify against him after he was arrested?" Rachel asked disbelievingly. "Do you really think the courts would award custody to a convicted abuser?"

"Tell me. Would you risk losing a four-year-old and a two-year-old to a violent father and a system you couldn't trust? No woman can trust the legal system. Not entirely. You ought to know that considering what's going on with Amy right now."

"I don't know." Rachel sat down on the bed beside him, her shoulders sagging. "I admit, I have a hard time putting myself into other people's shoes. That's why I direct. I'm not good at assuming roles." God. Why was she telling him her deepest thoughts? Great sex must make her tongue loose. "After it all went down, did his parents seek custody of them?"

"No. They washed their hands of Carrie and the kids. Blamed them for the whole thing. Like a couple of little kids had anything to do with it."

"Real charmers," she said dryly.

Harlan huffed a laugh. "The worst. The Abernathys are a discussion for another time." He turned to face her, his expression solemn. "What we need to talk about is if last night was a one-night stand, a nice but never to be repeated evening, or if we want to take it, this, us any further."

Rachel raised an eyebrow. "We need to decide this morning?"

"Yeah, we do. Last month I made the mistake of thinking you wanted to explore what's between us when you didn't and got in trouble at work for it. I don't want a repeat. I want to know before walking out of here if you want to take it any further."

"Which would mean?"

"Seeing me again. Going out with me. Dating me. More nights in the same bed. We share something special, despite your doubts about me because of my past. I'd like to see where this might take us. And yeah, we need to decide this morning. We work together and I need to know walking in Monday morning... Hell, walking in there tonight what our relationship is. I don't want to walk out of here thinking you want something you don't and then say or do something out of line at the theater. I need the job too badly."

"You don't want me walking out of here and going home and thinking about it?"

"Yeah. I don't want to walk out of here thinking you want to go forward and have you go home and think twice about who you spent the night with."

Rachel glared at him. "I know damned well who I spent the night with. I thought about it the whole way over here and I still got in bed with you."

"You did. So, Rachel? Do I thank you for a lovely evening and kiss you once more to say good-bye, or are you willing to go out with me again next weekend? Keep on seeing me? Try to build one of those things called a relationship? You know what I want. I don't know what you want. Your call."

She took a deep breath. "You realize we're both asking to have our hearts broken."

"I do." He leaned forward and kissed her lips lightly. "We disagree on some mighty important things. But we might find in the long run, those things mean less than the special something we share. The question is, do we have the courage to give us a go and find out? I'm in if you are."

Rachel didn't like being put on the spot. She liked to deliberate. But, she had to admire him for being so straightforward, and practical. He needed his job, and she didn't want any more lectures from Cameron and Josh.

But, shit. They were risking heartbreak. But no man in her entire life had ever made her feel like Harlan did. It wasn't all about the sex. Far from it. He reached her on a fundamental level, no man had ever reached before. It was worth the risk. *He* was worth the risk.

If she got her heart broken, so be it.

"Okay. I'm in. Let's do it. Let's see one another and find out where it might take us."

He leaned forward and captured her lips in a kiss both passionate and tender. "I'll do my damnedest, Rachel. I want to make it work with you."

To her surprise she meant it when she said, "I do too."

She followed him to the truck and gave him directions to her house.

As she changed her clothes and made up her face for lunch, she thought they were taking a hell of a chance. Ray Castillo's daughter and the ex-con. It was hard for her to fathom, but she'd agreed and she had no intention of reneging.

She had to be out of her mind.

A relationship between her and Harlan had disaster written all over it. But they would take it as far as they could and see where things went.

And hope they could avoid almost certain heartbreak.

Chapter Fourteen

Harlan

Harlan rocked back on his heels and stared in the window at the glittering display of baubles in the mall jewelry store. Beautiful, every one of them, but so far out of his price range it wasn't funny. Not that he had anyone to give diamonds to anyway. Evie was a tomboy and never wore anything remotely resembling jewelry. Carrie lived in scrubs and pulled latex gloves on and off all day. No rings and bracelets for her. And he didn't see a single thing anywhere near Rachel's style. As pretty as it all was, someone else would be the one to part with their precious dollars and take home the diamonds.

He walked on, savoring the ambiance in the large, upscale mall, and the simple pleasure of being able to come here. The meeting with his PO had gone well. She was a tough but fair-minded woman who despite her gruff exterior seemed to be on his side. He'd outlined his progress at both his jobs and suggested she bring her grandchildren to see *The Addams Family*.

Now in its fourth week, it played to sellout crowds and the board, which according to Rachel, made an unusual decision to run it through New Year's, rather than close it the week before Christmas. Which pleased him enormously. He was saving every penny of his light board money, and even after paying for Christmas gifts, he'd have enough to pay for another course at the community college. He might even have enough for a down payment on the used pickup truck one of Miguel's carpenters wanted to sell.

He glanced down at his cell phone. He still had a couple of hours before he was due at the theater and the only person on his abbreviated shopping list he'd taken care of was Nathan. Rather than gift him with something he might not like, Nathan was going to find a gift card to his favorite arcade under the Christmas tree. Evie would probably appreciate a gift card as well, he thought as he took a sharp right into the bookstore. She loved to read and a little spending money for books would likely be welcome. He'd priced an electronic reader and found it a bit more than he could afford this year. Maybe next year. Or for her birthday. He took a few minutes to look around the bookstore and by the time he was ready to check out, he'd decided there were some things here that would please Carrie, so he made it easy on himself and got them both a card.

Now for Rachel. He went back into the crowded mall. It was the last-minute rush before Christmas, but the shoppers were still mostly smiling and cheerful despite the pressure. Children and parents were lined up halfway across the mall to talk to Santa, and young and old alike were admiring the fifteen-foot-tall Christmas tree made of potted poinsettias. Unlike so many other things that'd changed drastically while he was in prison, Christmas at the mall was the same as it had ever been.

Except for the challenge of finding the perfect gift for Rachel. She didn't wear much jewelry, and what she did wear tended to be more wooden beads and woven bracelets than gold and silver. Her clothes were simple, but bright and colorful with eye-catching hues nodding to both her African and Native heritage.

He checked out a couple of women's boutiques but backed out of one when he got a load of the price tags and the other when he realized the workmanship was shoddy. He was starting to get worried and wondering if he needed to ask Amy for advice when he walked past a kiosk selling leather goods. There was a bit of everything, from tooled wrist bands to fancy belts to handbags and duffels. He took a belt off the hook and examined it. The piece was well made and attractive, but he'd never seen Rachel wear a belt. The wrist bands were okay but he'd seen her in better. The hats were nice but not something he felt confident choosing for her or any other woman. He'd better keep looking.

He was about to walk on when the young woman working the next kiosk stepped over. "Can I help you?" She smiled engagingly.

"I'm looking for something for my girlfriend. I'm kind of lost."

"Most men are. Describe her in ten words or less and I'll see what we can do."

He thought then said, "Exotic. Black hair, brown skin, gorgeous face. Great bod. Loves color. Beautiful woman."

"I wish my boyfriend described me like that," she huffed. "Are her tastes exotic as well? Simple leather or studs and fringe? Tooled or plain? Big handbag or small?"

He tried to remember her bag. "Maybe a little adornment on a purse." He bit his lip. "I don't know if you can help me. All her purses have those side zippers."

Her eyes widened. "*Oh*. Actually, we do have one with side zippers." She went into the storage drawer and dug around a minute before unearthing a caramel-colored bag in plastic wrap. "Here. Take a look at this one. It's even on sale."

He removed the purse from the plastic and turned it this way and that. It was mostly simple but for the fringed tassel pull on the upper zipper. He peered inside and then looked at the side pocket flanked by a zipper on either side. The space between the zippers seemed plenty roomy to him, at least as big as the pocket in the bag she carried now. He looked at the price and winced. "Lovely piece, but I don't think so."

"Let me calculate the price with the discount before you give up." The girl's fingers flew over a small calculator on the counter. She quoted him a second price that was far more reasonable. "I went ahead and took forty percent off since it's for your girlfriend."

He smiled at the girl. It would be a bit of a stretch, but he could get it at the new price. "You got a deal."

She gift bagged the purse and he counted out the money. Smiling like a fool, he hopped into his truck, grimacing at the ping that grew louder by the day, and headed on to the theater. He was working another show this afternoon, the Academy production for the middle schoolers. He'd been impressed by the abbreviated version of the play put on last week by the elementary school aged kids. "This is good. But wait until you see what the older kids can do. They'll blow you away," Miranda had assured him. He'd suggested Carrie bring Evie this afternoon with an eye to getting his niece involved in the Academy, but whether they would show up was anybody's guess.

Carefully, he slid the handbag under the seat and checked twice to make sure the doors were locked. He was a bit early, so rather than go straight to the auditorium he detoured through the office wing with hopes of snagging a kiss or two before he went to work. Sure enough, Rachel's door was open and her light was on. He stuck his head in the door and was rewarded when she motioned him in with a smile. "Shut the door and lock it," she said softly. "I need my Harlan fix."

He pushed the door shut until he heard the telltale snick and turned the lock. He stepped in and she came around the desk. They wrapped their arms around one another and came together for one of their bone-melting kisses they never seemed to get enough of. They touched and kissed and caressed each other for long minutes before he raised his head and grinned. "The longer we do this, the better it gets."

Rachel nodded. "Doesn't look like it's wearing off any time soon."

He grinned and adjusted the front of his jeans. It'd been almost a month since they'd spent their first night together, and the passion between them had gotten stronger as the weeks flew by. They'd gone back to the motel a couple of times, but Rachel had declared it an unnecessary expenditure and said his apartment and the futon were comfortable. So they'd taken to spending their nights together curled up on the folded-out futon. If the preacher or his wife noticed Rachel's car out front, they never said anything. Between his growing relationship with her, living in his own place, and the steady work with the theater and with Abonce Construction, his life was definitely looking up these days.

Rachel gestured to the minifridge behind her desk. "You have time for a roast beef sandwich and a soda? *Abuela* always packs way too much."

"Don't mind if I do. I was shopping and never got lunch."

"You didn't get breakfast either, unless you ate after I left."

"Bowl of cereal. Big whoop."

He sat across from her and she shared her grandmother's considerable spread. They were almost done when knock came, and Harlan got up to open the locked door. A couple of tweens stuck their heads in the door. "Hello, Miss Rachel," they chorused.

"Come on in, ladies." Rachel smiled affectionately at the girls. "You need to meet the man who designed the wonderful set you're acting on this afternoon."

The girls trooped in and Rachel introduced them as Angela and Monique and said they were best friends, which surprised him because the girls seemed so different. They announced they were about to become sisters and chatted about their parts in the play, then ran out to get ready.

"Lovely girls, but best friends? I wouldn't put them together in a million years," he said.

"That's okay. Nobody puts us together either," a cheery voice said from the door. "But we go together and so do they."

"They're about to become sisters. I hope they keep getting along," a deep voice added.

Harlan turned around to see an adult version of Monique holding the hand of a tall, straight-backed man who had retired military written all over him. Rachel's face broke into a huge smile. "Jake, Marci, come in. You need to meet our new set designer. Harlan, these are the parents of the young ladies you just met. Jake and Marci, this is Harlan. He designed the *Addams Family* sets."

Jake whistled under his breath. "We saw those sets last week when we came to the adult production. Fantastic work." He offered his hand. "Glad to meet you."

"The sets are wonderful. I love them!" Marci enthused. She turned to Rachel. "Well, we're gonna do it." Her face was wreathed in the happiest smile he'd ever seen.

"Okay, I'll bite. The girls said something about becoming sisters?" Rachel asked.

In response, Marci thrust her left hand in front of Rachel. A gorgeous rose-shaped ring crusted with pink diamonds graced her finger. "The wedding ring will fit right under. It'll be big enough to wear by itself because this one will have to come off at work. But it'll go back on the minute I get out of there."

Harlan looked from Jake to Marci. These two were getting married? *Ooookay*.

Rachel was warm and sincere in her congratulations. "So when's the big day? Spring? Summer?"

"Would you believe next Sunday after the eleven o'clock worship service?" Jake asked. "We'd do it up fancy, but we need to get it done, the sooner the better."

"No, not even," Marci laughed when Rachel and Harlan peeked at her stomach. "Dr. Esquivel is selling the clinic and moving to Brownsville. He offered us the opportunity to buy in and we have a better chance of borrowing the money if we're married. It's a dream come true for both of us. Marrying and having a share in a clinic we run."

"Before you ask, we can hire a doctor to come in and supervise," Jake added. "Sign off on the paperwork while we practice medicine."

Harlan and Rachel offered additional congratulations and the happy couple disappeared. He sank down in the chair, his earlier good mood dimmed.

"What's wrong?" Rachel asked quietly.

Harlan smiled crookedly. "I'm happy for them. But it's kind of a reminder of how far behind I am. I was going to have my degree and be a baseball coach by now. That's totally off the table."

"Right."

He sighed. "Don't mind me. I knew what I was doing when I blew the bastard away. But it sucks sometimes, you know?"

"There's still a lot you can do." She smiled encouragingly.

"I know. I need to figure out what." He laid a light kiss on her lips. "Speaking of, gotta go earn my tuition money."

She reached out her hand and he gave it a squeeze. "You'll figure it out."

She held his hand for a minute and he could see she didn't want to let go. "Better get going," she whispered. "The lights aren't on in the auditorium yet." He nodded. "Would you rather have burgers or the Fruteria between shows?"

"Burgers are fine. We can go to the brand-new café down the block."

"Works for me."

He dipped his chin, left her office and cut through the stage to the auditorium. Backstage was a flurry of activity, with tweens and young teens scurrying around. He hustled to the light board and turned on the lights. The lobby was already filling with parents and other tweens and teens, presumably family and friends of today's cast.

He spotted Josh and his niece Beth escorting a venerable old lady on a walker. Cameron followed with Miguel and Miguel's wife, and two more wealthy looking older women. Miguel motioned him over and introduced him to Josh's *Bubbe* and Cameron's mother and aunt. Josh's nephew Jackson was playing Fester and the entire Abonce-Heiser-Goldstein clan had come to see his Durango debut.

"I was in the show last week," Beth announced proudly. "I was Grandma Addams."

"That was you under all the ugly?" Harlan asked.

"Sure was," she said with a big smile.

The family moved on and he stared after them wistfully. Another bunch who had achieved a lot. The Heiser family owned Heiser Steel, Miguel owned his own company, and Josh's family owned a string of successful clothing stores. Not that Harlan wanted to do any of those things, but he'd wanted to achieve something.

You made the choice, his inner voice reminded him. He'd opted to do what he did knowing full well what the consequences would be.

Get off your ass and make a decision about your direction. You can still achieve a lot, and you'd better, if you want to hold on to Rachel.

Yeah. He needed to suck it up. And think about the woman who'd laid a sweet kiss on him not a half an hour ago.

Things were going in the right direction, but they were far from perfect. They never talked about her father, and they were both careful to steer clear of any mention of Carrie or what he'd done to Cole.

Rachel had expressed her opinion of his sister once, and once was more than enough. She was a woman with strong opinions. It was a miracle she'd changed her mind about a relationship with him. He didn't expect her to change her mind about Carrie. To her way of thinking, Carrie was responsible for what had happened. But Rachel didn't understand. She'd never seen the bruised, terrified, beaten down woman his sister had become.

Rachel was strong and self-assured and would never let a man abuse her like Cole had done to Carrie. Rachel would never understand the woman Carrie had been, and to some extent still was, despite the progress she'd made while he was away.

Miranda called the one-minute mark and he started lowering the lights when Carrie and Evie came in. They waved at him and one of the student ushers escorted them to a couple of chairs a few rows from the back. His mood sweetened considerably. Maybe he and Carrie could get Evie involved at the Academy. He knew it was expensive, but Rachel had often spoken of the many scholarship students attending. It would be so good for Evie to be exposed to something other than the less than stellar neighborhood and school where she was growing up.

More than once he'd thought maybe Carrie wouldn't've been so dazzled by Cole and his money if she hadn't grown up so poor. Maybe it would inspire Evie to aim a little higher than Carrie had done.

If he could do something about Rachel's opinion of Carrie, and vice versa, it might smooth things out and make things easier between all of them. The ladies had both passed judgment based on a little knowledge and a lot of opinion. They needed to sit down and get to know one another. He and Rachel could ask Carrie and Evie to join them for burgers between shows. Rachel could tell Carrie and Evie all about the Academy. Carrie had her doubts about enrolling Evie and Rachel would be the perfect salesperson.

Unless the production this afternoon sold it. The show the kids put on was out of this world. Evie's eyes were shining when they met up with Harlan in the lobby afterwards, where the cast was accepting well-deserved congratulations and the girls were holding bouquets. "It was wonderful." She beamed even as Carrie looked around uncertainly at all the well-dressed families. "Do you really think I could do something like that? It would be awesome."

"Sure you could," Harlan said cheerfully.

"Evie, no." Carrie shot him a look. "No way in hell can I afford something this grand."

"Of course you could, with the kind of scholarships they offer," Harlan said. He returned Carrie's look with one of his own. "And here comes the lady to convince you." He motioned to Rachel. "Rachel and I are going out for a quick bite between shows. You and Evie can come with us and she can tell you all about it."

Carrie's eyes widened at the sight of Rachel striding across the lobby. "I didn't realize she was so pretty."

"She's definitely a beauty." Rachel approached them with a smile. "Rachel, I'd like you to meet my sister Carrie and my niece Evie. Carrie, Evie, this is Rachel."

Was it his imagination, or had Rachel's smile slipped a bit? Her expression was welcoming as she turned to Carrie. "I'm glad to meet you. Welcome to the Durango." Carrie murmured her thanks. Rachel then turned to Evie and her smile widened. "Did you enjoy the production?"

"It was stupendous," Evie near shouted. "Uncle Harlan said I could maybe come to the Academy."

"Evie, I don't think so," Carrie said.

Rachel's eyebrow shot up. "Goodness, why not? We'd love to have her."

Carrie turned a deep shade of red but she said nothing.

"And ladies, that's why I took the liberty of inviting Carrie and Evie to join us for burgers," Harlan said quickly. "Rachel, I'd like for you to tell Carrie and Evie all about the Academy and what they...we-can offer her."

Rachel smiled graciously.

"Certainly. I'd love to." She checked her watch. "We'd better go now. We have to be back in plenty of time for the evening production." She motioned to the front door. "Shall we?"

Chapter Fifteen

Harlan

The air was brisk but not overly cold as they walked the block and a half to the new coffee shop that'd opened last week. Evie peppered Rachel with questions all the way. Carrie was mostly silent, and Harlan was beginning to wonder if asking them to come had been the best idea. His sister was easily intimidated by successful women, and Rachel had successful written all over her. Hopefully, the ladies would connect on some level while eating a hamburger together.

It was early and the little café was mostly deserted. They requested a booth near the window. He and Rachel took one bench, leaving the other for Carrie and Evie. The eager young waitress took their order, and Evie returned to her nonstop questions for Rachel, who answered with kindness and enthusiasm. "The Academy kids do a lot of the same productions the adults do, but not all of them. Sometimes we have to make a substitution."

"Why?" Evie demanded.

"Because some of what we do is a little too grown up for folks your age. The same reason your mom doesn't let you go to R rated movies. So we do something else, something your mom would let you see."

"What are some of the shows the kids do?"

Rachel answered obligingly and was describing a recent Academy reprise of *Oklahoma* when their burgers arrived. Harlan tried to draw Carrie into the discussion, but his sister was obstinately quiet, even when he brought up the possibility of Evie getting a scholarship. Rachel patiently explained the application process to Carrie, who said nothing but a noncommittal "We'll see."

He couldn't understand. He thought Carrie had gotten stronger after Abernathy's death. She'd certainly been assertive enough the day he rented his apartment, and he knew she wanted good things for her kids. But maybe she hadn't changed as much as he thought.

Or maybe the way she felt about Rachel was the problem.

If it was, he didn't have the vaguest idea what to do about it.

They finished eating and he took care of the check. Carrie and Evie walked with them to the end of the block. "We're parked over there." Carrie pointed to a side street leading into the neighborhood. She turned to Rachel without really looking at her. "Nice to meet you."

Rachel smiled graciously. "Likewise. I enjoyed meeting Evie as well."

His sister and niece took off for their car and he and Rachel headed up the sidewalk. "Your niece is darling. So personable." She said nothing about Carrie.

"Thanks." He hesitated for a moment. "Did you like Carrie too?"

"Sure. A little quiet, but a nice lady. I liked her fine."

Rachel wasn't a good actress. She was lying through her teeth.

So much for the ladies connecting.

The evening show was outstanding, as usual. Amy's eyes were dancing as she watched the last of their enthusiastic audience walk out the door. "You know I'm starting to get lonely on the weekends," she teased.

"Sorry about that. Your other sister's still gone?" he asked.

"She graced us with her presence for an entire forty-eight hours a week and a half ago and then she was gone again. She said she'd be home for a few days at Christmas and some in January. If it were me, I'd be thoroughly sick of the traveling by now, but she doesn't seem to mind."

"What about Leshawn? Has he come back?"

"No. He's vanished. They've tried to pick him up, but he hasn't been at any of his known addresses, haunts, or girls."

"I don't know whether that's good or it's bad," Rachel said as she came up beside him. "Maybe he finally got the message."

"We can only hope," Amy said with feeling.

"More likely he's waiting to catch you off guard. I don't mean to be a wet blanket, but assholes like Leshawn don't give up. It took me beating the crap out of him to get him to lay off my cellmate."

"It's a miracle you didn't get in trouble for it," Rachel said.

"Leshawn didn't let on. He didn't want it known he got the shit beat out of him by a white guy. Anyway, don't let your guard down, either one of you. Go get out of costume and I'll walk you to your car before Rachel and I take off."

After they saw Amy safely away, Rachel followed him to his apartment and met him at his front door. They fell into one another's arms, barely making it in the door before they were all over one another. He'd have thought, as often as they had been together in the last month, the passion would have cooled. But it was hotter than ever, and only getting better as they learned one another's bodies, likes and dislikes.

Rachel liked to make love fast and furiously the first time and savor him the second and third time. She loved when he went down on her and happily returned the favor. Sex up against the wall wasn't to her liking, but she loved the shower. She now knew he liked being on top or the bottom, but he insisted they be face to face. He wanted nothing even remotely resembling what one of the other prisoners had tried with him once.

He and Rachel had each paid a visit to the doctor, and since both had clean reports, and Rachel on birth control, there'd been nothing between them for weeks.

They left a trail of clothes between the front door and the futon. He jerked it into a reclining position and they tumbled down together, their kisses and touches on fire as they stroked one another until all he wanted was in.

Rachel parted her legs and pushed his butt closer. "Now," she demanded against his lips. "I want you now. We can do the slow and easy later."

He entered her with a single stroke, burying himself to the hilt. She gasped and moved beneath him, drawing up her legs to give him maximum access. He withdrew almost to the tip and pushed into her again. "Harder," she murmured. "I won't break."

He didn't have to be told twice. He pushed into her again, harder, and they set a fantastic punishing pace. They moved together, the futon creaking beneath them as they held nothing back. He was vaguely aware of her fingernails clawing his back, and there would probably be bruises on her arm. But neither cared. All that mattered was the heat they generated and the depth of passion as they spiraled toward a hot, hard climax that had them both gasping for breath.

He rolled off her and went to the bathroom to get a warm washcloth. He came back and gently cleaned between her legs. "Great being bare," she hummed as he tweaked her before throwing the washcloth on the floor.

"In more ways than one." He kissed her temple. "Give me a minute before we go for round two."

She nodded. He held her and kissed her, leisurely kisses at first, but as his cock hardened and her nipples pebbled, they became deeper and more consuming. Determined not to rush things, he took his time, kissing his way down her body to the sweetness between her legs. He'd learned what she liked here as well, his tongue rasping over her clit the way she loved until her back bowed her off the futon with his name on her lips. "Again," he demanded as he sought her sweetness again, and a third time before he moved over her and entered her for the second time.

He'd meant to go slower, but a sense of urgency overcame them, desperation almost, and he hammered into her as hard as he had before. Her movements were hot and frantic, giving and demanding at the same time. They soared like a rocket, coming together in a fiery blaze that had them both screaming. When she came, her body trembled as his orgasm pulsed within her. When the throbbing stopped, he withdrew and laid beside her, his hand on her stomach. "Good for you?" he asked as his hand moved in circles on her heated flesh.

She nodded. "Good for you?"

"The best."

They hadn't asked each other that since their first time together.

He offered her a midnight snack and they finished off a small carton of ice cream. He started to say something about Evie and the Academy, but he hesitated. Rachel had been less than impressed with his sister and had lied about it rather than tell him the truth. Which was fine for this evening, sparing them an argument neither wanted to have, but dishonesty about something so important wouldn't work in the long run. No relationship could survive without issues being faced and dealt with. He sighed inwardly as they curled up on the futon and pulled a blanket over them.

As wonderful as the sex had been tonight, there had been a barrier between them that had never been there before. The urgency, the unbridled passion... It seemed they both had been trying to get past the invisible barrier, but it hadn't gone away.

He pulled her close and wrapped his arms around her. The sex hadn't made a difference. All the wild sex in the world wasn't going to make it go away. The only thing that would lower this particular barrier was complete, unvarnished honesty. The kind of honesty that would make them or break them.

The kind of honesty he wasn't willing to risk tonight, and he doubted she wanted to risk it either.

He didn't know when they'd be willing to take the risk to find out if what they had was strong enough to hold.

Chapter Sixteen

Rachel

Rachel didn't know whether to feel empathy for Carrie or feel sorry for her. Neither emotion really suited. She should be angry with her.

But after meeting the woman, she couldn't bring herself to be angry or contemptuous.

Maybe Carrie really was that weak.

And if she was, she didn't deserve Rachel's disdain.

Rachel got out of Amy's car and the sisters trudged to the front door. The afternoon performance had gone well and Granny's fried chicken dinner had been out of this world. But they were tired and glad for the few days off.

Christmas was only four days away and she and Amy were both off work until the day after Christmas. Then one more weekend of *Addams Family* and Amy's commitment would be over. January would be slower for Rachel as well, with the next production, which she wasn't directing, not beginning until the first week of February.

She was ready for some downtime. Between her commitments at the theater and the time she spent with Harlan, she was tired. And her lack of sleep last night wasn't helping. Harlan had dropped off quickly, but she'd lain awake for hours, seesawing between her confused feelings about his sister and troubling unease about their future as a couple. There'd been distance between them last night. The sex had been spectacular. It always was. But it had been tinged with an urgency borne of the very real fear their relationship was headed for serious trouble in the form of his sister.

It was clear he loved the woman. He would have to, considering the sacrifice he'd made for her. But from what she could see, Carrie was weak and unable to stand up for herself. A failing that'd seriously damaged her brother's life. The question was: could Carrie have stood up for herself or was Harlan enabling her?

Which made Rachel crazy. She didn't do weak and she didn't do enabling.

Amy unlocked the front door and froze. "Shit, damn, and hell," she snapped. She backed from the door and shook her head. "Don't go in. The house is trashed."

"*What?*"

"You heard me. It's a disaster in there and we don't know if whoever did it's still inside." She turned to Rachel, pure terror on her face. "We need to get in the car and lock the doors until the police get here."

They sprinted back to the car. Rachel's fingers trembled as she dialed 911, then Officer Falkner. Within ten minutes there were three cruisers at the house and Officer Falkner pulled in five minutes later in his private vehicle. "What's going on?" he demanded.

"They've already cleared the house. Whoever did this is long gone. Not that we don't know who did this," Amy said, her voice trembling.

"Well, shit. This has Leshawn Hayes written all over it," Falkner said grimly. "Have you been back inside?"

"They told us to let them work," Rachel said, "and we could come inside when you got here."

"Okay, ladies. Let's go take a look."

The three of them stepped into the house. One of the patrol officers met them in the kitchen. "He got in through a sliding door in the sunroom. Looks like he used a crowbar."

"What've you found?" Falkner asked.

"Not a whole lot of actual damage. More like things were tossed and thrown around, drawers emptied, cushions on the floor, stuff like that. Shampoo and dish soap poured all over the kitchen and bathrooms. Oh, and a message on one of the bedroom mirrors written in lipstick. 'Castillo family better watch it.'"

Amy turned to Rachel. "Now he's threatened our whole family. What about our grannies? They're old. They're defenseless."

"I know. I'll call them right now." Rachel turned to Falkner. "Why is he still loose? I thought you said his parole would be revoked."

"We can't find him," Falkner admitted. "Like I told you last week, he's in the wind and has been since he confronted you last month. He hasn't reported to his PO and hasn't been anywhere we've looked. And we've looked. Not making his parole appointments bought him a bench warrant. A lot of cops are looking for this guy." He glanced around. "The forensic folks are on their way. Let's take a look around before they get here."

It was pretty much what the young officer described. Not much in the way of damage. More a mess it would take them hours to clean.

Rachel's clothes were yanked out of the closet and her dresser drawers, and thrown on the floor. Same with Felicia's stuff. Most of Amy's underwear was missing, including several sexy panty and bra sets. "He remembered them." Her sister's face turned red. "I should've gotten rid of them a long time ago."

"Surely he doesn't expect you to wear them for him again," Rachel gritted out.

"He may." Rachel and Amy looked at Falkner in horror. "He's not rational. He's never been rational, but he's escalating. He's doing things that'll get him thrown back in jail and doesn't care. Clearly, he thinks if he gets your attention, you'll go back to him." Falkner motioned to the room. "That's what all this is about. Getting your attention."

"He certainly has it," Rachel said grimly.

It took the CSI team hours to process the entire house. It was well after midnight before they trudged out to the front porch, where Rachel and Amy waited with Falkner. "Whoever did this left nothing behind to ID 'em," the lead investigator told them.

"We know who did it," Rachel ground out. The CSI and wandered back inside and they followed.

"So what's next?" Amy asked as she returned the cushions to the living room sofa.

Falkner looked frustrated. "We redouble our efforts to find him. Warn your family of the threat."

"What about a protective order? Or would he walk right through it?" Amy asked.

"No point with him going back to jail the minute we see him. We don't even need tonight. He was already in violation of his parole before this." He looked at Rachel. "Are you carrying?"

"I am. How'd you know?"

He gestured to her purse. "It's pretty obvious. Just be careful with it." He turned to Amy. "You?"

"No, but I wish I was."

"I wish you were, too," Falkner said.

Whoa. Rachel hadn't expected to hear that.

"So what now?" Rachel asked.

"We'll keep looking for him. You stay alert and stay safe. And you ladies do your damnedest to have a good Christmas in spite of all this, you hear? Give your mother my love. How is Lorene, anyway? I haven't heard from her in years."

"Doing well. Remarried and living in Houston."

"Glad to hear it."

They thanked Falkner and Amy saw him out.

"So much for sleeping in," Rachel said tiredly. "We'll have to get this mess cleaned up, and I still need to hit the grocery store. Mom sent me a list of stuff we need for Christmas dinner. Not that I'm in the mood." Their mother was coming over to their house on Christmas Eve and she and her daughters would cook Christmas dinner in their kitchen. Which meant they had to get the place cleaned up tomorrow before they hit the grocery store.

It took the entire morning to set the house to rights and have it ready for guests. They'd try to have happy holidays, but the situation hung over them, dampening their trip to the supermarket with their mother's lengthy grocery list in hand. On top of all the Leshawn crap, the situation with Harlan continued to bother her. She didn't know which would be worse, avoiding the conversation, or admitting her true feelings about Carrie. Both had the potential to bite her in the butt.

They'd almost finished shopping when the bakery put out big boxes of donuts iced in Christmas colors and so fresh they were still warm. "Damn. I wish the theater was still open. We could treat everyone to a holiday donut," Amy said.

"The theater's open today and tomorrow. The Academy's having a big Christmas party tonight and Josh is manning the box office and selling tickets for the after Christmas performances. Some of the others may be working. Put 'em in the basket and I'll take them by later this afternoon while you hit the lingerie department."

They finished their mammoth shopping chore and unloaded the groceries. Rachel left Amy wrapping gifts and headed to the Durango. The streets were clogged as they always were around the holidays and it would take her twice as long as usual to reach the theater.

She was halfway there when she remembered Harlan's gift, a black leather bomber jacket, wrapped and waiting to be delivered. It would take too long if she went home for it. Besides, she didn't know if he was working today. Maybe she could slip away sometime in the next day or two and spend a little time with him. She'd started to invite him to Christmas dinner, but this was the first Christmas with his family in almost ten years, and he would want to spend the day with them.

There were several cars in the parking lot, including Harlan's truck. She could hear voices coming from the Academy rooms, so she stopped there first and left one box of donuts with Jessica and the moms helping her with the party. "I'll take a spin through the office and bring you whatever's left," she volunteered as Jessica and the women got to work on the donuts.

Josh was hanging up the phone as she stepped in his office with the second box. "Here you go. Whatever you don't want goes back to the Academy."

"Oh, you beautiful woman," he crooned as he took three donuts from the box. "I missed lunch. But it was worth it. Friday night's already sold out and Saturday's nearly there. I was answering the phone by nine this morning. Unlike some of us, who got to sleep in."

"Damned if that's so," Rachel complained. Harlan stuck his head in the door and she motioned to the box. "Here, enjoy. I didn't realize you were working today."

Harlan took two donuts and killed them in a couple of bites. "I came by for a little while. I took some measurements so I can have a set design ready to go for *American Idiot*. I'll need to start the minute the crew clears the *Addams Family* furniture pieces." He chewed the last of his donut then looked at her. "So why didn't you get to sleep late this morning? You said you would when you left here yesterday."

"Getting a jump on Christmas dinner?" Josh teased.

"No. We spent the morning cleaning up the house. Leshawn broke in yesterday afternoon and trashed it. Stole all of Amy's underwear. She's out trying to replace some of it."

Harlan and Josh's expressions changed to alert and hard. "Her asshole ex came back," Josh said flatly. "I thought he was in the wind."

"He blew in long enough to toss the house and make a mess," Rachel said, "then disappeared again."

Harlan's jaw muscles were working overtime.

"Scary," Josh said. "I thought his goose was cooked when she filed the stalking charges."

"He doesn't care about the charges or anything else." Harlan shook his head. "You and your sister honestly think filing charges is gonna stop a shit like him?"

Rachel's chin came up. "It beats sitting on our asses and doing nothing. Now the minute they see him, they'll pick him up and take him to jail. If nothing else, it gets his parole revoked."

"Then it's a good thing she went ahead and filed," Josh said quickly before Harlan could say anything. "If you want me to, I can walk these over to the Academy after I eat a couple more. I need to go make an appearance and thank the volunteers."

"Sure. Merry Christmas. No, wait. Happy Hannukah?"

Josh smiled. "Whatever you want to wish me. For the first time in my life, I'm going to Christmas dinner. Betsy Heiser informed me in no uncertain terms I was welcome to be Jewish every other day of the year, but as Cam's husband I'd better be by his side at the Heiser family Christmas dinner or my name was mud. And her grandchildren better be there as well. Bubbe's not pleased, but I'm not about to piss off my mother-in-law."

"So you're gonna gag down some of her delicious turkey and spectacular dressing. I feel so sorry for you," Rachel teased. "Happy Whatever and I'll see you on the twenty-seventh."

She exited the office with Harlan by her side. "The charges she filed. It's not gonna do anything but piss him off," he said as she strode toward the door.

She turned to him with her eyebrows raised. "When did you get to be such an expert on stalking laws? When did Carrie file charges?"

"She didn't. She knew it wouldn't do any good, particularly against a dick like Abernathy. Same goes for Amy. Leshawn's gone to ground and he'll stay there until he decides to do something else. It's not gonna make one damn bit of difference."

"If they pick him up, they'll take his ass to jail," she snapped. "Leave it be, Harlan. I'm tired and in no mood to hear about Leshawn. Amy and I aren't kidding ourselves. We know nothing's foolproof. We know it's not gonna stop him if he insists on coming back. But they can pick him up if he shows his face. At least Amy's trying. Your sister never did one damned thing to protect herself."

Harlan gasped and glared at her. "That's a shitty thing to say about a woman you don't know."

"You're right. I don't. But you have to admit for whatever her reasons, she did nothing. Maybe if she'd done something, *anything* to stop the son of a bitch, you wouldn't have lost ten years of your life. Maybe she *is* that weak. If she is, she has my sympathy. But the bottom line is you had to fight her battles, and you wound up in prison. I'm sorry if the truth pisses you off. It damned well would me."

They glared at one another. So much for avoiding the conversation. She'd spoken the ugly, unvarnished truth as she saw it. From the look on his face, he wasn't happy with her and he didn't bother to hide it.

Now the question was whether their relationship would survive the honesty.

Right now, it didn't look like the odds were in their favor.

Chapter Seventeen

Harlan

Harlan seethed as he stared at Rachel. "You have no business judging Carrie," he spat. "You weren't there. You didn't see what he did to her, the terror she lived in because of him. You've never been in a situation like hers, so you don't know."

"What do you think's going on at my house? He threatened our entire family. He scared us to death."

"And you think it wasn't worse for Carrie? She had children she was trying to protect. Your sister doesn't have any children in the mix."

"No, we have two grandmothers to think about. He threatened a couple of octogenarians who can't defend themselves. Amy is in damned near same position your sister was, but she's choosing to handle it differently, and you don't need to make me feel bad that she is."

"There's a helluva lot of difference in threatening children and threatening adults."

"Not really. The grandmas are helpless. Look, what's done is done as far as your family's concerned. But we're in the middle of it and we're taking what steps we can. Amy's going to do all she can to stop the SOB. At least we're trying, which is more than Carrie did.

"You're so judgmental it's amazing you can get through a day with exploding. Your view of the world—black and white, right and wrong—is so fixed in stone you don't see that *everyone's* lives are shades of gray. I should've known you'd judge Carrie. It's what you do."

"What the hell did I say that's judgmental? Maybe your sister really couldn't stand up to him. Maybe you did have to do what you did. I don't know. One thing I'm sure of is we're doing everything we can to put him behind bars. I shouldn't have to apologize for that." She turned on her heel and marched out before he could reply.

Fuck. Harlan stomped back to the stage and snapped out his tape measure and took the rest of the measurements. He shouldn't be surprised. At her core, Rachel was sure she knew best how people should behave, and she had passed judgment on his sister for being weak. Abernathy had done serious damage to Carrie's fragile spirit. Damage so deep, even when Abernathy was dead and forever out of the picture, Carrie was still fragile. She'd live with what he'd done to her for the rest of her life.

Damage Rachel would never have let a man inflict on her body or her soul.

And there it was in a nutshell, he thought he drove the wheezing old pickup through the heavy pre-Christmas traffic. Rachel couldn't understand because neither she nor Amy would've put up with Abernathy's abuse. No woman who packed heat like Rachel did would be afraid of a man's fists. It'd taken Amy awhile to smarten up when it came to Leshawn, but she was stronger than she had been, and she has Rachel at her back.

He whipped into line at a drive-through taco joint and placed his order. Well, they'd had their moment of honesty. He knew what she thought of his sister and she knew exactly what he thought of her attitude. Now the barrier had become a yawning gap he wasn't sure they could bridge. He was afraid his relationship with Rachel was crumbling in a way they'd never be able to put it back together.

Maybe they should've kept their mouths shut. But what kind of relationship would they have when there was a list of topics they could never discuss.

Damn it to hell. He folded out the futon and lay down, staring across the room at the little Christmas tree Carrie and Evie insisted he needed.

He'd looked forward to this Christmas for years, and until today he'd thought it was going to be a good one. But if his relationship with Rachel was crumbling, not so much. Despite her being too judge-y and hardheaded, she'd come to mean something to him.

Merry Fucking Christmas.

***

Harlan sat on the floor leaning against Carrie's sofa. The living room was filled with discarded bows and torn wrapping paper, all that was left of the pile of gifts gracing the bottom of the tree when he'd arrived this morning. Carrie had outdone herself. Each kid got several gifts, and there were a number of presents for him. He'd commented on the expense, and she'd reminded him the children had outgrown Santa and said she gave them extra gifts to make up for what Santa no longer brought. He wondered if the Abernathys would relent and send something, but Carrie assured him it would be a cold day in hell before they did anything for Cole's children. They hadn't seen their grandchildren in years, and there was no reason they'd change their minds anytime soon.

The gift cards he'd purchased had gone over well, and he promised the kids an outing to the mall sometime in the near future to use their cards.

He didn't know if he'd give Rachel her gifts. He hadn't seen or heard from her since their fight at the Durango. He hadn't reached out to her, and he hadn't expected her to reach out to him. But he'd thought plenty about the shit she'd flung at him, and the more he thought about them, the more depressed he became. It'd been all he could do not to call Carrie with an excuse and turn over in bed and sleep all day. But she'd chattered for a solid month about how happy Christmas was going to be this year now that he was out of prison and their family was reunited. It didn't feel reunited, with his mother dead and Joe in Mexico. But he'd be damned if he burst his sister's balloon. She'd had too much bad in her life for him to be a dick about Christmas. If she wanted to be happy about the season, he'd be there with her.

He plastered on a smile and went to the kitchen where he found Nathan struggling to get the turkey out of the oven. "Want me to get it?" he asked the boy.

Nathan shrugged and handed Harlan the hot pad holders. He put the turkey on the counter in the space Carrie cleared. He got the pan of dressing out of the oven, sniffing appreciatively. "Mom's recipe?" he asked.

"She taught me the last Christmas she was alive," Carrie said. "I didn't want to bother, but she told me you loved her dressing and the only way you were ever going to get it again was if I made it for you. So I practiced every Thanksgiving and Christmas I wasn't working, and here it is."

He smiled though his throat had closed up. "Thanks for learning." He peeked at the pots on the stove. "Her sides too?"

"A couple. I switched out the sweet potatoes for green bean casserole. The kids like the casserole better."

"Super. So do I."

Evie and Nathan set the table and made the tea while he did the honors with the turkey, which was large enough to feed them for a week. The meal was delicious. Their celebration was happy and sad at the same time.

He was happy to be out of prison and to be reunited with his sister and her children, and delighted to be eating the holiday meal he'd dreamed of every Christmas for years. At the same time, it was bittersweet eating the meal his mother always prepared without his mother and Joe at the table with them. Those holidays had always been so wonderful, with hope and joy and love in abundance.

They still had the love: he, Carrie, and the children. He was trying, not too successfully, with the joy.

And the hope. He would make it, he promised himself. He'd deliberately and willingly suffered a setback, and his dreams about his future were gone. But he was out now and free to make of his life what he would. He'd power through and his life would become one he could be proud of. It was going to be hard, harder than he'd first realized, but he wouldn't give up.

The kids put their dirty dishes in the dishwasher and Carrie told them they could go. "Gotta try out those new computer games." She winked and Harlan laughed. He pitched in and together they put away the leftovers, with Carrie insisting he take home two or three meals worth of food, which he'd be delighted to do. He packed a huge plastic container of turkey and gravy and more containers for the sides.

"I really appreciate all the goodies," he said as he put them together in a sack in her refrigerator. "I've been doing the drive-throughs way too often lately."

"And the coffee shop down from the theater?" she asked.

It reminded him of the evening with Carrie and Rachel and his face fell. "Not really."

He tried to perk up, but his sister had seen right through him. "You're not as happy as I thought you would be," she said quietly as they sank into the sofa. "I thought you'd be thrilled to be out of prison and starting a new life. You seem down. Want to talk about it?"

"Not especially."

Carrie looked at him, then asked, "Does it have anything to do with a certain gorgeous woman you haven't mentioned today?"

His eyes narrowed. "I said I didn't want to talk about it."

"Maybe you need to," she said softly. "You haven't been yourself since you walked in here. I'm guessing something went wrong with her. Maybe talking about it would help."

"Nothing's gonna help," he insisted.

"What did she say to you?"

"A lot of things," he told her before he could stop himself. "I said some things too. Things we both would've been better off not saying."

"Such as?"

"I told her the charges her sister filed were worthless and they were kidding themselves if they thought it would help. She said it beat doing nothing and—" He clamped his mouth shut.

"And I should have done the same," she finished. He nodded. "Does she realize what I was up against? Does she have any concept of what Cole would've done to me and the children if I'd crossed him?"

Harlan sighed. "That's part of what we fought about. She says her sister's ex is as dangerous to their grandmothers as Cole was to the kids, and they filed charges anyway. So no, she doesn't understand."

"She sounds like a hard-ass."

"She kind of is. And she's strong. She doesn't take shit off anybody. Hell, she carries a gun in those fancy concealed-carry purses."

"Then she wouldn't understand." Carrie's lips trembled. "What else did she say that has you so upset?"

"Nothing."

"Bullshit. What did she say, Harlan?"

"She thinks if we'd done things differently, I wouldn't've lost ten years of my life."

"She thinks it's my fault," she said. "She said that too. Didn't she?"

"Yeah, she did."

Carrie's eyes filled with tears. "It *is* all my fault," she whimpered, "for getting involved with him in the first place. But I didn't know, honestly I didn't. Not until it was too late and I couldn't get out. I had the kids to protect. I ruined your life and I'm so, so sorry." She put her face in her hands and sobbed quietly.

"Please don't cry. It wasn't your fault, it really wasn't. My life's not ruined, it's just going to be different now." He wrapped his arms around her and pulled her close.

"Then whose fault was it?" she murmured.

"Cole Abernathy's," he said firmly. "And nobody else's. You had no choice and neither did I."

But more and more he was beginning to wonder if there had truly been no choice, or if there had been other options he and Carrie could have exercised.

Chapter Eighteen

Rachel

Rachel sat at her desk with the manuscript of *Evita* in front of her. It was a tantalizing possibility. The story would appeal to a wide audience and the music, particularly the signature 'Don't Cry for Me, Argentina,' was well liked. It would be easy to cast. *Too easy*, she thought as she went down the listed parts. With only five main characters, there would be too few roles to fill from a rapidly growing talent pool. Unless the ensemble was huge, there'd be a lot of disappointed actors and singers. But she wasn't ruling it out.

She put it to one side and picked up the manuscript for *Memphis*. Lots more characters here, and the heavily black cast requirements would give the Durango a chance to feature their increasingly diverse talent. *It would give them a chance to showcase her sister again*, she thought before she could stop herself.

She'd always known Amy could sing and act, but now, after doing *Addams Family*, Rachel knew how immensely talented her sister was. Being in the play, especially in the lead role, had been good for Amy. Directing her had been a pleasure, and a show like *Memphis* would give them a chance to work together again.

Josh was smiling as he stuck his head in the door. "I just sold the last ticket to the weekend performances." He did a fist pump in the air. "Another healthy chunk of revenue."

"Awesome. Tell me, are we anywhere near digging out from the financial hole created by the pandemic?"

"Not yet, but we're getting there. Maggie roped in a couple of good grants in December, and the Navarros bestowed as they always do, God bless 'em."

"Which I'm sure pleased Maggie to no end."

"The grant, and the knuckle-knocker she finally let Kirby put on her finger. She's on cloud nine over the engagement. They're planning a summer wedding." He snickered. "She really made him work for it."

"She needed to. But it's been a while, and he seems to be okay these days. I'll make it a point to congratulate her the next time I see her."

Josh sailed out and Rachel's smile faded. She was glad for Maggie. If anyone deserved a happily ever after with a man who loved her, it was hard-working, sweet-natured Maggie. But it brought home to her the sad state of her own love life.

She and Harlan had a lot of chemistry, but they had some serious issues separating them. Issues so serious she didn't think they'd ever achieve a meeting of the minds. She would try. This morning she'd seen him sitting at the table in the breakroom busily sketching something on a large piece of paper. She'd wait until lunchtime and see if he wanted to get something to eat with her. The Fruteria, maybe, or the coffee shop. It would give them a chance to talk and maybe clear the air. It was going to be damned hard to get past the things they'd said, but she was willing to try.

How Harlan felt about it was another matter altogether.

One thing he'd said was probably true: the stalking charges. Leshawn probably didn't even know about them. He was still nowhere to be found, despite the best efforts of SAPD. According to Falkner, he hadn't shown up to any of his known residences or hangouts, and even his former associates and a couple of reliable snitches didn't know of his whereabouts. His grandmother said she had no idea where he was. She said she'd kicked him out weeks ago for getting high at her place.

Rachel wasn't sure she believed his grandmother, but whatever. She and Amy were looking over their shoulders everywhere they went. They'd spent most of the holiday trying unsuccessfully to persuade their grandmothers to hang out in Houston with their mom and Harold for a week or two.

She and Felicia went to the gun range and the two of them had blown holes in life size targets for an hour. Felicia offered to stay a few extra days, but Amy wouldn't hear of it. "You have a job and a life. You don't need to stay here and babysit me." Reluctantly, Felicia had flown back to wherever this morning, and Rachel was sorry to see her go.

She gave herself a mental shake. Brooding wasn't going to make her problems go away. She read through *Memphis* and earmarked it for probable inclusion somewhere in next year's lineup. She was reading through *In the Heights* and practically salivating at the possibilities when she heard a tentative knock on her door and looked up. Carrie was standing at the door looking at her uncertainly. Here to have lunch with Harlan, no doubt.

So much for clearing the air over lunch. She'd have to talk to him later.

Rachel arranged her face to a pleasant expression. "Harlan's working at the end of the hall in the breakroom. Three doors down."

"Actually, I came to talk to you."

"Good," Rachel said briskly. "Evie will love the Academy. I'm glad you've decided to let her come."

Carrie shook her head. "That's not why I came. I wanted to talk to you about Harlan."

Oh, shit. This was not going to go well, especially if she was honest with Harlan's sister. She would be as kind as she knew how to be. But at the same time, she'd explain what she and Amy were doing and why. Maybe Carrie would come to her own conclusions.

Rachel forced herself to remain pleasant. "Come in and have a seat."

Carrie sat and clutched her purse strap nervously. "I... I don't know where to begin."

"Wherever you want." She stared at Carrie and wondered what this woman would say.

"I guess you know what happened. I was being abused by my boyfriend. Evie and Nathan's father. I couldn't do anything about it. Harlan shot him. He saved my life."

"Okay." Rachel waited patiently.

Carrie sat up straighter. "If Harlan hadn't killed Cole, he would've come to the hospital and killed me. Shot me, strangled me, smothered me. I'd be dead today. Harlan did what he had to do." She stuck out her chin defiantly.

"I see. So you believe there was no other solution than for Harlan to shoot Cole."

"There wasn't," Carrie snapped. "You have no idea what Cole was capable of. He would've killed me if I'd crossed him. He would've taken away the children and done who knows what to them. Harlan said you think I should've done something. Don't you understand? I *couldn't*. You have no business judging me. You have no business judging him either. You weren't there. Since you don't have a clue what went on, you need to keep your mouth shut."

"What makes you think I'm judging you?"

"Well, aren't you? Harlan said you fought with him about it."

"I did fight with him. But that's between us."

"He said you didn't understand. He said you were strong and wouldn't've let anybody push you around. That's fine for you. But you don't get it. I'm not strong like you. I couldn't stand up to Cole. I couldn't. You've never been in the position I was in, or you wouldn't be so high and mighty about what Harlan and I did."

"No, I've never been in the position you were in. And I'm not trying to be high and mighty. But I'd have to say my sister's in a similar position with a no-good ex stalking her. The first thing she did was call the police, and we've done everything we know how to help the process along so they can take care of the problem. I get you were scared of *Cole* and you felt helpless. But Amy's scared too, for herself and for our elderly grandmas. She feels just as helpless as you did and she's still pushing to have it resolved legally. I'm trying to understand, but it's difficult."

"You think I should've done something. You think because I didn't, Harlan paid the price." Carrie shook her head. "That's what you think, isn't it?"

"What happened with your family, it's over and done. We're handling things differently, and you coming in here and getting into it with me isn't gonna change anything."

"I thought if I explained it to you, maybe you'd understand and not fight with Harlan. Maybe you'd understand why he did what he did. But you don't and you never will."

"I understand he did what he did to protect you. I understand you were terrified out of your mind. But I don't understand why you did nothing. For Harlan's sake I wish I could."

"I see I've wasted my breath. Damn. I did the best I could. I'm sorry if that doesn't change your mind." Tears poured from her eyes as she jumped from the chair and ran from the room.

Rachel rubbed her fingers across her forehead. Harlan's figure filled the door. From the look on his face, he'd overheard most or all of what they'd said. "Was that really necessary?" he snapped. He glared at Rachel through squinted eyes, his brow down and his jaw muscles jumping. "You didn't have to say those things to her. She tried to explain."

"Say what things to her? It's all right for her to read me the riot act and I'm not supposed to tell her what I think? I don't think so. Harlan, I was as gentle as I knew how to be, but I told her the truth. I don't understand, but I didn't fuss at her. I pointed out Amy's in a similar position and doing everything legally possible to stop what's going on. Your sister didn't like hearing it."

"There you go again. You have no idea what hell Abernathy put her through. You have no idea how beaten down and scared she was. You think because you and your sister are strong, everyone's supposed to be as strong as you. Well they aren't. Carrie's not. And it's time you stop faulting her for being who she is."

"Damn it, I wasn't passing judgment. I was careful not to. I tried to be kind and understanding. She was frightened of him, I get it.

You think we're not frightened? Amy's scared out of her mind and so am I. But she's still doing what she can to stop him. Am I so wrong for thinking maybe Carrie could have done *something*?"

"Maybe what Carrie could or should've done is none of your damned business."

Rachel took a breath. "You're right. It isn't. The Burke family dynamics is absolutely none of my business and I'll be certain to stay out of it from now on."

She stared at him a minute as her heart crumbled into little pieces. So much for them sitting down at lunch and talking things over. She cursed the tears forming in her eyes. "It's hopeless, Harlan. You and me. We see things too differently. You think I'm cruel and judgmental and I—" She stopped and bit her lip.

"Go on and say it," he demanded harshly.

"I think you killed a man you didn't have to kill to protect a sister who should've taken steps to protect herself." Her eyes swam with tears she willed not to fall in front of him. "Damn. I thought we might... Hell, it was hopeless from the get-go." She looked up at him, not trying to hide the pain. "I'm sorry. I'm really sorry."

"So am I. But if you refuse to see our point of view, maybe it's for the best."

"It's not that I refuse to see your point of view. I understand where you were coming from. You were trying to protect your sister. If Carrie is so weak she couldn't protect herself, okay. I believe it, but I don't understand it. Here's something for you to think about. You're all pissed off because you think I'm refusing to see your point of view. But it doesn't seem like you've exactly knocked yourself out to see mine. You've never even asked me about Daddy."

He turned on his heel and stalked out. She waited until he was down the hall before she put her head in her hands and let the tears fall. Maybe he was right. Maybe she was hopelessly judgmental. But she thought he was wrong, and he and his sister refused to face the truth.

Deep into her cry, she almost let a phone call go to voicemail and would have if it had been anyone else's ringtone. But Amy was calling. She picked up the phone and clicked it on. "Whatcha need?" she asked tiredly.

Her sister mumbled something incoherently. "What? I can't hear you."

"I said he raped me," Amy whispered. "He came here to the house and he raped me."

Rachel felt the blood drain from her face at the same time her stomach sunk to her knees. She bit back a string of curse words. "Is he still there?"

"N...no. He's gone."

"Are you sure?"

"I heard him drive away."

"Call the police. I'm on my way."

She threw her phone in her purse and ran to her car, shoving Harlan aside as she passed him in the hall. Her fingers trembled on the steering wheel as she peeled out of the parking lot and ducked and dodged her way through the heavy Christmas traffic. *Damn him. Damn the son of a bitch to hell.* He must've broken in. Never in a million years would Amy open the door to him. He must have broken through the front windows. Or maybe he came in the sliding doors again. It didn't matter how the fucker had gotten in. He'd hurt her sister.

She pulled onto their block, slowing and looking closely at the cars parked along the street, and breathed a sigh of relief when she recognized all of them. She pulled up in the driveway behind Amy's car and sprinted for the front door. To her surprise the front window was intact. *Shit.* He must've come through the sunroom.

The front door was unlocked. She took out the Ruger and eased inside in case Amy was wrong and he was still in the house. She looked around and gasped. This time the damage was severe. The living room was in shambles, with the television smashed and the coffee table splintered and bloodstains on the sofa. Their treasured picture of their father was crumpled on the floor, the frame broken, and Felicia's prized collection of first edition books was ripped up and scattered on the floor.

Rachel didn't stop for a further assessment of the damage. She took a quick look in the kitchen and a quicker one in the sunroom, expecting to find a broken window and glass on the floor. It too was untouched. *Well, hell.* He must have broken into one of the bedrooms.

She'd figure it out later. She needed to find Amy.

Cautiously she made her way down the hall, checking each bedroom. No sign of forced entry here either. He wasn't in the house. Breathing a sigh of relief, she put the gun back in her purse. The bathroom door was closed and locked. *Smart.* Her sister had the presence of mind to lock herself in. "Amy, it's me. There's no one else here. Open the door."

The door opened a few inches and Rachel stared in horror. Amy was weaving on her feet, her left eye swollen shut and blood running from her nose. Her lip was split, and her clothes had been practically ripped from her body. She was bent over, cradling her stomach. "I think he broke my ribs," she wheezed.

"*Amy,*" Rachel breathed. "Let's get you to your bed."

She took her sister's arm and gently walked her to her bedroom. "The police should be here by now. Did you tell them what happened?"

"*No.* No police." Amy looked at her in alarm. "You can't call the police."

Rachel looked at her disbelievingly. "What do you mean, I can't call the police. He *raped* you. He beat shit out of you. You have to report it."

"I... I can't," she mumbled. "He'll kill Granny. He has her address. Said if I didn't let him in, he'd go straight to her house and kill her. Said if I told, he'd kill her and *Abuela*. He'll do it, too."

"You let him in?"

"What was I supposed to do? Let him kill Granny?"

"You call Granny and tell her to get out of the house. Now, you're gonna call the cops and report this."

"But...but—"

"You don't report it, he'll be back. Over and over and over. Like Cole Abernathy did. Now, I'm gonna call. Okay?"

Amy nodded numbly. Rachel called nine-one-one. Ten minutes later, Officer Falkner, arrived with an older policewoman he introduced as Officer Diaz. The policewoman immediately sat down beside Amy with a notepad and began coaxing the story out of her.

Rachel followed Falkner to the trashed living room. "Did you touch anything in here?" he asked.

Rachel shook her head. "The only thing I've touched is Amy. She's in such bad shape she can hardly walk."

"Officer Diaz called for an ambulance." He sighed. "I feel terrible about this. I'd feel bad about any woman, but one of Ray's girls? This is awful."

"You tried your damnedest to find him and couldn't."

"No. But now when we do find him, the additional charges on top of the stalking and breaking parole means he won't be out for a long, long time. She intends to press charges, right?"

"She better. But it scares me. He threatened to hurt our grandmothers. She let the SOB in the door because he threatened to kill Granny. He has her address."

"If I were you, I'd get your grandmothers out of town for a few days. Make whatever arrangements you need to while I call forensics to come to the house. Then you can answer my questions."

She called both grandmothers and told them to pack a bag for a trip to Houston, no arguing. Their mother said she and Harold would be there by late afternoon to get the grandmothers.

Then Falkner had questions for her. She was answering his last question when an ambulance pulled into the driveway. Officer Diaz directed the paramedics to Amy's bedroom. "Your sister took quite a beating along with the rape," the policewoman said. "I'm not a medical professional, but I've seen enough of these cases to know she'll be in the hospital for a few days." She looked around the room. "The house is a crime scene and will have to be vacated until the evidence techs have gone through it. You have somewhere you can stay?"

She immediately thought of Harlan, and dismissed the thought just as quickly. "I'll manage."

"You don't want to be here if he decides to come back. It might take us a few days to find him."

What a peachy thought. "I'll stay in a motel."

"Good idea."

Rachel packed enough clothes to last a week. The paramedics emerged with Amy on a stretcher and told them what hospital they were taking her to. The policewoman turned to Officer Falkner. "I'll follow her over and finish taking her statement. I'll take the rape kit straight downtown afterward."

"She said she'll press charges, didn't she?" Rachel asked anxiously.

Officer Diaz looked at her with a ghost of a smile on her face. "After I got through talking to her, she was more than ready." She and Falkner did a fist bump.

"Officer Diaz has a way of helping women move from fear to anger," he said solemnly. "She excels at it."

"God bless you, ma'am," Rachel breathed.

She threw her suitcase in the trunk and followed the police car to the big county hospital. Amy was in the emergency room, and Rachel sat down with a clipboard and took care of the paperwork.

It was over an hour before they let her in to see Amy. Officer Diaz was perched on a stool beside the gurney with a notebook and a pencil. "I'll write up your statement this evening and bring it by for you to sign in the morning. Both of your statements." She turned to Rachel. "Due to the extent of her injuries, the docs want to give her a head-to-toe physical, including X-rays and a CT scan, as well as a couple of days of observation and some antibiotic IV's. She's torn up pretty bad and was exposed to God knows what in terms of infection."

"The bastard," Amy said through her split lips.

"You got that right," Rachel added bitterly.

Officer Diaz took the bagged rape kit and left. Rachel sank down onto the stool beside Amy. "I'm so sorry," Rachel murmured. "I guess we should've left the house."

"I never really believed he would do something like this. Boy, was I wrong." She tried to sit up. "Shit. Even breathing hurts." She looked at Rachel anxiously. "What about Granny? *Abuela*?"

"Lie down. Mom texted a few minutes ago. They're already halfway here. The grandmothers wanted to come see you before they left but I told them you were in a bad way and didn't need any more commotion. I told Mom she could come in for a few minutes but we needed her to get the grannies out of town. Is that okay?"

"I don't want to see anybody. Not even Mom. I'm dirty. Nasty." Her eyes filled with tears.

"We'll get you in a shower as soon as you have a room."

"Not what I meant."

"I know what you meant. But a shower will help. A good therapist will help too. Will your insurance pay for it?"

"I don't know."

"I'll find out tomorrow."

Amy was quiet then asked, "Felicia?"

"She's fine. Already in wherever. I texted her but told her not to come. She's safer where she is."

"Damn. What about you? You should go to Houston. You need to get out of the house. You're not safe there. You'd be safer at Mom's."

"Somebody needs to be here for you."

"You need to go. Please. I'm gonna be in here awhile and you don't need to sit around a damned hospital."

"You'll need me when you get out. I'll get a motel room," she said when Amy started to object again. "I can't go back to the house anyway. It's a crime scene."

"Aw, shit." She looked miserable. "Is the sofa history? Maybe it can be cleaned."

"Don't you think it would be better if you never have to look at it again?" she asked gently. It was obvious from looking at the bloody sofa what had happened there.

"I guess so."

She shut her eyes, then they popped open and she gripped Rachel's arm. "What about the play? I can't do it like this and at the Durango there's no such thing as an understudy."

Oh, shit. It was sold out and the theater desperately needed the revenue. "I guess I'll have to do it," Rachel said slowly. "There's nobody else. I won't do it as well as you do, but—"

"You'll do fine. You have a whole three days to get ready." Amy tried to laugh and then grimaced. "Shit, it hurts."

Rachel swallowed hard. She couldn't take seeing her sister in pain.

It took another hour for the hospital to admit Amy and move her to a room. Their mother arrived about six. She was horrified by the damage done to her daughter but held it together admirably during a short visit, waiting to break down until she left Amy's room. "I should stay," she said through her tears. "My baby needs me."

"Mom, I'll be here for Amy. We need you to get Granny and *Abuela* out of town. He'll hurt them if you don't."

Her mom shook her head. "How...why did she ever get involved with him in the first place? I taught her better."

"She was trying to get away from him," Rachel reminded her mother. "She told him over and over to get lost and he wouldn't leave her alone. The only reason she opened the door today was because she was terrified of what he'd do to Granny if she didn't. Don't fault her for it."

And there it was. Rachel had no business faulting Carrie. Amy was a lot stronger than Harlan's sister, yet she'd done the same thing for substantially the same reason.

Rachel cringed and pushed the thought from her mind. But the unsettling realization remained with her as she sat with Amy a little longer. It nagged her as she let herself in the Durango to get a copy of the *Addams Family* manuscript and pick up take-out tacos for dinner.

It continued to haunt her while she checked into a motel on the opposite side of town from where they lived.

It inserted itself into her brain while she was trying to learn Morticia's dialogue, making it damn near impossible to memorize the lines.

She was beginning to think Harlan was right. If Carrie had been subjected to years and years of abuse, then maybe she really had been beaten down so badly she couldn't stand up to Abernathy. It seemed more likely every time Rachel thought about it. Not something she'd understood, but now... It made more sense than she would've   believed.

Chapter Nineteen

Harlan

Harlan threw open the back door and strode into the Durango. He was a little early, but traffic had been lighter than he'd thought it would be on New Year's Eve. Every New Years in prison he'd imagined what it would be like to be out partying and drinking in the new year. Now here he was, his first New Years out of the pen and he was working a show. At least he was getting paid for it. To a person, the cast had agreed to give up their New Year's celebrations and come in for three extra shows, and they weren't getting a dime. Maybe he would go down to Thirties afterward with the cast and celebrate a little. Or maybe not, if Rachel was going to be there. He had no desire to be anywhere near her. He was angry and hurt, and unlike most of the Durango crowd, he wasn't a good enough actor to hide it from her or anyone else.

He would be better off going home and watching the ball drop on TV.

By himself.

He didn't want to be around Carrie, either. He wasn't angry with her for attempting to talk to Rachel, but he felt too raw to talk about it. He'd not spoken to her since the debacle earlier in the week, and she hadn't contacted him either.

He hadn't seen Rachel since she'd knocked him out of the way running for the door. Which shouldn't surprise him. He'd finished the sketches that afternoon and spent the rest of the week on a job for Miguel's company. She wasn't necessarily avoiding him, but she hadn't gone out of her way to seek him out.

A part of him was fine with it. He was still angry with her for not trying harder to understand Carrie. But then, maybe he'd been guilty of not trying to see her point of view. He'd never even asked her about her murdered father. And the part of him who'd fallen hard for her missed her terribly. A part of him wanted to sit down with her and try to work through their differences and convince her they should try again.

Maybe she was right and it was hopeless. But they ought to give it at least one more shot before walking away.

The women's dressing room was empty but for Amy. She was already in costume and was going over a copy of the manuscript. Odd. She had her lines down pat and had since the earliest rehearsals. He started to say hello but decided to leave her be since she'd surely heard what happened and was probably angry on Rachel's behalf.

The crew was setting up as usual. They seemed unusually subdued. Normally they were cheerful and smiling, but tonight their faces were solemn and a bit anxious. The same for the volunteers working the snack bar. A sober faced Miranda was whispering to her boyfriend behind the souvenir counter and whatever she told him had him looking horrified.

Something was wrong.

He paid for a soda and a sack of popcorn and finished them off before heading to the light board. Noel came in a few minutes later and was his usual smiling self, so whatever was wrong, he didn't know about it either. The audience was cheerful, laughing and talking, and glad to be here. Maybe nothing was wrong. Maybe it was his imagination. They'd give these extra performances and make their much-needed money, and Monday he could start building the *American Idiot* sets.

He put on his headset and heard Miranda call "twenty minutes." She came over to the board and parked on her stool. "Lights and sound, headsets off. I need to talk to you privately."

He and Noel removed their headsets and moved closer. "We have a situation I need to make you aware of." She glanced toward the stage. "Amy's not going on tonight."

"She's not?" Harlan blurted. "I saw her in the dressing room not fifteen minutes ago. Already in costume going over her lines."

Miranda shook her head. "The Morticia you saw isn't Amy. It's Rachel. She's going on tonight in Amy's place."

Rachel? Rachel was under the skin-tight costume and outlandish wig? "Why?" he demanded. "Where's Amy?"

Miranda bit her lip. "She's in the hospital. This isn't for publication, okay? But the ex raped her. Beat the daylights out of her. They're still running tests. She may have suffered internal injuries along with broken ribs and a beaten face."

"Raped?" Harlan mouthed.

Miranda nodded. "I have never been so appalled and horrified in my life. Everybody I've had to tell is sick about it."

"No shit," Noel said darkly.

Harlan's throat burned and his hands were fisted at his sides. Leshawn deserved to burn in hell right next to Cole Abernathy. "Do you know if she pressed charges?" he asked.

"She did, but he's still hiding and they haven't picked him up yet," Miranda said. "Now, about tonight. Rachel's going on. She's never done the role and has had a whopping three days to learn the lines and the songs. She and Eric practiced the dance this afternoon, so she at least has it under her belt. If she misses a line or a cue, don't let it throw you. If there's any way you can employ your magic back here to cover a gaffe, feel free to use it. I've already talked to the cast and they're prepared to cover her any way possible. The crew's taped sheets of dialogue on some of the furniture where it can be concealed. Rachel's a real trouper and with everyone's help she'll pull this off. If I see anything for you to do or change, I'll tell you, so listen for it."

"Will there be an announcement ahead of time?" Noel asked.

"I don't know what Josh wants to do. He's here to do the welcome spiel Rachel normally does."

She turned her mic on and announced time. They put on their headsets. Harlan's heart thumped and his head spun. His palms stung from his nails digging into them and his fingers felt numb as he worked the light switches. He tried not to think about the pain Amy was suffering. He tried not to worry about how unsafe Rachel was. She wouldn't be safe until Leshawn was picked up, and maybe not even then. Cole had been out in three hours. With Leshawn's drug money, he probably had an attorney who'd get him out every bit as quickly.

The Castillo sisters wouldn't be safe unless or until Hayes was put away for good.

If he was put away. The law didn't always work to protect the victim. Harlan knew that all too well.

It hadn't worked for Carrie. It might not work for Amy even though she pressed charges. She might not be believed. Which, incredibly, happened.

Then there were the upcoming performances. Shit. Rachel was good. Great, even, but not a miracle worker. He didn't see how she could perform a major role with a scant three days' notice, especially since she was worried sick about her sister.

No wonder nobody was smiling tonight.

Miranda called the one-minute mark and Josh started toward the stage. He gave the usual welcoming spiel and then announced the substitution, cleverly making it sound like Rachel's performance would be an enormous treat for the audience.

Harlan lowered the lights, the orchestra began the prelude with a flourish, and on the darkened stage the ensemble took their places.

Slowly, he raised the lights on the family cemetery and the production commenced.

They were ten minutes in when he decided Rachel was a miracle worker after all. She had the songs down perfectly. As for the dialogue, he noticed her checking the lines in front of her once or twice, but she was so subtle the audience wasn't going to catch on.

He caught a couple of minor gaffes in the second half, but nothing the audience would notice. When the show was over the cast enjoyed the usual applause and kudos from the audience. Someone, probably Josh or his husband, presented Rachel with a bouquet of beautiful white roses, and she was beaming as she took her place with the other actors in the lobby.

Miranda switched off her headset and collapsed on her stool. "Okay, now I can breathe again," she said.

"She did it," Harlan said. "She did it exactly like Amy. I don't know how she could do it so perfectly."

"She spent most of the last three days holed up in her office with the script and her laptop in front of her, going over the videos of our production," Miranda said.

Troopers all of them. The show had gone on, and Harlan was amazed Rachel was able to put her feelings for her sister aside to do this for the Durango.

Miranda called them all together afterwards, and Rachel was treated to a hearty round of applause from the cast and crew. Miranda thanked them all for a job well done and dismissed them. "It's New Year's Eve. Go celebrate," she told them.

Most of the cast scurried for the dressing rooms. Rachel slumped in her seat, clearly exhausted.

He sat beside her. "You did a great job."

She smiled faintly. "Thanks."

They sat quietly for a couple of minutes. "After you get out of the costume, I'll see you to your car."

She looked at him in surprise. He motioned to the stairs. "Go on. I'll wait."

The cast and crew had scattered while Harlan waited patiently outside the women's dressing room. The door was ajar as it always was, but he turned the other way to give Rachel and Sasha, who was also taking her time, their privacy. Sasha came out first and wished him an unsmiling "'Night." Rachel joined him a couple minutes later. She'd changed into jeans and an old tee and had cleaned off the garish Morticia makeup, making her look washed out and even more exhausted.

They walked out the back door and Rachel locked it behind her. Theirs were the only two cars in the parking lot. The only other car in the vicinity was an ancient Mustang with darkened windows parked across the street. They looked at one another and froze. "Do you know that car?" he murmured.

Suddenly the old Mustang roared to life and jumped the curb into the parking lot, coming to rest between them and their vehicles. "Oh, *shit,*" Rachel breathed. "Call nine-one-one *now.*"

He whipped out his phone, one eye on the car. The driver's side opened and Leshawn leapt out, a long knife in his hand. "Hey, there, little sistah. I come to talk to you," he taunted. He waved the knife in front of him. "Got a warning for you and your bitch sister. I'm not through with you and I'm not through with her. She calls the po-lice, I'm gonna carve her up but good. I'm gonna carve her up and carve you up. Work on your grannies a little as well. So she better back off, you hear me? And you, Burke. We still got a score to settle. So that better not be the po-lice on the other end of the line."

Rachel looked at Leshawn with contempt. "Fuck you, Hayes."

Leshawn's eyes widened and he rushed them. Harlan started to grab for Rachel when a trio of gunshots peppered the ground in front of Leshawn's feet, stopping him in his tracks. "Don't come one fucking foot closer," Rachel ground out in a tone he'd never heard her use. "Nice try, asshole. Harlan, do you have nine-one-one yet?"

He looked down at the gun in her hand. Terror shot through him. *This could end badly on so many levels.*

Leshawn stared at her gun disbelievingly. "You wouldn't."

"Hide and watch."

Rachel and Leshawn continued to stare at one another. Harlan kept an eye on Rachel as he made the call. The dispatcher told him to keep the line open. "We'll record everything he says," she said.

Harlan held up his phone. "They're listening, Hayes," he said tensely.

Leshawn looked from Harlan to Rachel and started to back away. She delivered two more shots to the ground next to his feet. "You're not going anywhere. I'm not looking over my shoulder for you for one more damned minute. Throw away the knife. Face down on the ground. *Now.*"

He back up another foot and she shot the ground again. "I'll do it, motherfucker. *Down.*"

He tossed the knife to one side and lowered himself to the asphalt. Harlan held his breath. He had no idea if or how many more shots Rachel had in her pistol, or if she'd really shoot the SOB and if Leshawn would stay down on the ground. How damn long it would take for the police to arrive might affect whether she snapped like he had all those years ago and shoot Leshawn to put an end to it.

It seemed like forever, but it was probably less than five minutes before three squad cars roared up. The policemen surrounded them and Rachel dropped her weapon on the ground. She was shaking, her body vibrating.

"What's going on?" an older policeman demanded as a couple of burly cops jerked Leshawn to his feet.

"This man threatened us with his knife and I held him until you could get here. He raped my sister the other day. Beat hell out of her. She's still in the hospital."

Leshawn immediately started to buck. "I didn't rape nobody. Bitch is lying. She shot at me. For no damned reason."

"This what you call no damned reason?" A young policewoman aimed her cell phone flashlight at Leshawn's knife on the ground.

Rachel turned to the policeman, who was looking at her suspiciously. "My sister's already pressed charges. Call Officer Falkner. They've done a rape kit and everything. You'll find we're telling the truth."

Leshawn let out a furious howl. Rachel turned toward him, every pore of her body oozing hate. "That's right, asshole," she spat.

"She's in the hospital and they did a rape kit, which has your DNA all over it. With the injuries you left on her, plus tonight, you'll be so old by the time you get out of prison you'll need a walker to move."

Leshawn let out another furious howl and started fighting the officers, who cuffed him and shoved him in a squad car. Rachel's gun was bagged along with Leshawn's knife and spirited away.

"I know you have to question us," she said tiredly to the policeman. "Me and Harlan. I have a key to the theater if you want to sit down somewhere more comfortable than your cruisers."

The policemen preferred to question them in the squad cars. They were hammered separately for over two hours. He had a few bad minutes when his status as an ex-con on parole and his history with Leshawn was revealed, but the arrival of an Officer Falkner and Josh Goldstein to corroborate Rachel's explanation of his presence satisfied the officer's suspicions.

"No telling what Leshawn's going to say about me," he said to Officer Falkner. "I may be in the hot seat again tomorrow."

"Are your prints on either weapon?" the policeman asked.

"Only the phone. And the dispatcher was on the line until the cops arrived."

"Then don't worry about it."

The honking horns, firecrackers and other New Year's hoopla had died down by the time the police were finished with their interrogation.

The squad cars left one at a time. Josh had long since left, leaving Harlan and Rachel alone in the parking lot. He followed her to her car. In the pale glow from a nearby streetlight he could see her shaking hands. "That was certainly worth a boatload of nightmares," she muttered. She collapsed into the driver's seat. "Amy's going to have more, though."

"How'd you do it?" he asked quietly. "Stand there with a gun in your hand and not kill him? Didn't you want to?"

Rachel shrugged. "The thought crossed my mind."

"But you didn't. Even after what he did to your sister, you didn't."

"No. I didn't." She stared straight ahead and took a breath. "Scum like him isn't worth killing. We'll let the law take care of him." She laid her head on the steering wheel for a minute. "Thanks for waiting. I couldn't've made the phone call with the Ruger in my hand. I wonder how long before I get it back."

Harlan winced. "It may be a while."

"'S'okay. I have others."

Of course she did.

He shut the door and she backed out of the parking lot. He watched her go before getting in the truck and driving to his place. Pretty much everything was closed for the night, but he had a pizza he could nuke and a couple of beers he could finish off.

He chowed down and then lowered the futon to lay down.

Sleep was elusive and an hour later he sat up and reached for the refurbed iPad he'd sprung for at an after Christmas sale. He went on the Internet, hoping to entertain himself until he got sleepy. But the week's events kept going through his mind.

Amy. Brutally beaten and raped. Pressing charges against her attacker.

Leshawn. Threatening him and Rachel with the knife.

Rachel. Shooting the ground at his feet and holding him at bay until the cops arrived. Turning Leshawn over to the authorities for justice. Trusting justice would be administered. By the system, not by her or her sister.

They'd done things the way they were supposed to be done.

Harlan sighed and turned off the iPad. Amy had been brutalized in much the same way his sister had. But Amy had the courage to report the abuse and to stand up against her attacker and say, "no more." She gave the legal system the tools it needed to put him away.

Rachel could've shot Leshawn dead and gotten away with it. With the knife in his hand, he had put her life...their lives in danger.

Instead, she'd turned him over to law enforcement. She'd trusted them to deliver justice and protect her life and her sister's.

He couldn't undo the past, but he could reconsider it. And what he came up with deflated him.

He made a cup of coffee and pulled on a hoodie and went out on the landing. He sat on the top step and watched as the eastern sky slowly brightened from black to gray to the pink of a cloudless dawn. He sipped the coffee as he contemplated the inescapable truth.

He and Carrie had fucked up big time.

Carrie could've gone to the authorities early on. She could've filed charges and gotten a restraining order. She could've refused to put up with any more of Abernathy's shit. She could've given law enforcement the tools to take care of the problem.

She did none of it.

His choices hadn't been any better. Instead of calling the police, he could've leaned on Carrie, put her in the car and taken her to the police department. He could've stood beside her and made her to do what needed to be done. At the very least, he could've waited until Carrie was conscious and possibly willing to press charges before he took matters into his own hands.

Instead, he'd gone out, bought a gun, and taken a man's life.

And he'd pay for it every day for as long as he lived.

It was damned hard to swallow that he and Carrie had made bad choices all those years ago. But they had, and it was time to acknowledge it. It was time to go forward understanding they could've done things differently. If they had, Abernathy would've been the one sitting in jail and Harlan could've gone on with his life.

There was no going back. His life had gone off track and would never be what it could have been. He and Carrie would live with the aftermath of their mistakes for the rest of their lives. It was time to admit some of the fault was theirs. He needed to acknowledge the guilt he'd buried, and Carrie would have to admit she'd not been as strong as she should've been. He would have to be honest with her and hope she could live with the truth. He'd enabled her for far too long. He wasn't going to do it any longer.

He waited until the sun was well over the horizon and what little coffee remained was cold. He went back inside. It was still early, but Carrie was an early riser and would be up by now. He found his phone and her voice was hesitant as she answered. "Harlan?"

"Happy New Year," he said solemnly. "You busy this afternoon?"

"No."

"Good. No, you don't have to cook lunch. I'll bring takeout."

"Any reason you're coming over?"

"Yeah, I'm coming for a reason. We need to talk."

Chapter Twenty

Rachel

Rachel pulled into the driveway with a big smile on her face. "Wow, will you take a look? The Durango elves have been busy." The front porch and mailbox were festooned with balloons and brightly colored streamers, and "Welcome Home, Amy" was splashed across the front yard on a huge yard sign.

Amy laughed even as she teared up. "How lovely. They've been so wonderful. The cards, the flowers, and a box of fancy chocolates from Josh and Cam. They've gone out of their way."

"It's a bribe," Rachel said.

"Bribe?"

Rachel turned to her sister. "*Memphis.* You'd both have to try out, of course, but Josh and I were kicking around you as Felicia Farrell and Brian as Huey Calhoun. Him with his freckles and his red hair and all. Quite the visual contrast."

"Can't get much whiter than Brian." They both laughed. Amy clutched her chest. "Damn, it still hurts to laugh. Hell, it still hurts to breathe."

"At least you don't have any internal injuries. I was worried sick until they cleared you." She unsnapped her seat belt. "Come on. Let's get you inside and some lunch in you."

She went around to Amy's side of the car. She reached out to help, but Amy held up her hand. "I do better by myself." She bit her lip. "Jesus, I don't want to go back in there."

"I know. But it'll be all right."

"Yeah, sure. If I had a choice I wouldn't, you know." She hesitated in the middle of the sidewalk. "I don't know if I even can walk inside."

"Tell you what. Come on. Try. If you go in and are still freaked out, I'll take you wherever you want to go."

Rachel ran ahead and had the door unlocked and open by the time Amy eased her way to the porch. She stepped inside and froze in her tracks. "What the fuck?"

Rachel looked at Amy uncertainly. "I know it's still where it happened, but maybe now it won't hit you in the face with ugly memories every time you walk in the room." Amy said nothing. Rachel swallowed. "I hope it's okay. The *Addams Family* cast worked on it Sunday evening after the last performance."

Amy looked around in wonder. "It doesn't even look like the same room."

"I should hope not. We worked hard so it wouldn't."

Amy slowly circled the room, taking in the changes. The bloody sofa was gone, as was the matching chair and the smashed coffee table. In their place sat a beautiful new living room set in gray leather Rachel had chosen and Felicia had paid for. The new television was courtesy of Rachel's now groaning credit card.

Their mother had overnighted elegant new curtains from her favorite Houston department store. Their landlord had agreed to let them take up the bloody carpet, revealing a gorgeous wood floor Josh and Cameron worked late into the night to repair and polish. Letti, Kevin, and Eric had repainted the walls a pale grayish pink to set off the leather pieces.

John Marsh had taken the crumpled picture of their father and worked restorative magic, and Celia had framed three new copies, one for each daughter. Even Sasha had gotten involved, painstakingly sorting the pages from Felicia's books and arranging them in order so a professional bookbinder could rebind them. Amy looked at Rachel with tears in her eyes. "Who do I thank for doing what?"

"Sit and I'll make some lunch and tell you all about it."

Amy collapsed on the new sofa. "Comfortable. And welcome. The drive home wore me out. Stupid, huh? A thirty-minute drive and I'm ready to lie down."

"Do you want to rest first and eat later?"

"No, I'm hungrier than I am tired. Besides, if I go to sleep I'll dream about it again. It's okay," she added when Rachel looked at her in alarm. "The shrink said it was normal. Dreams, nausea, and depression. Plus, I still hurt like a son of a bitch and can't get comfortable. The happy pills help a little, but not much."

Rachel sat down across from Amy. They could talk a few minutes before she put lunch on.

"So what does the therapist say will help?"

"Time, mostly. And going back to my normal routine as soon as I can. Like anything will ever be normal again. I don't think I'll ever feel safe."

"Even with Leshawn locked away forever and eternity?" The judge had denied bail and based on Amy's extensive injuries the prosecutor was going for the maximum sentence.

"It'd be worse if he were loose, but I still don't feel safe." Tears filled her eyes and ran down her face. "It wouldn't have happened to you or Felicia. You would have shot him."

"Not if I didn't have the gun beside me," Rachel reminded her. "The important thing is you survived. You're still with us and you will heal. I'm not saying something asinine like 'it's gonna be okay' because it's not for a while. Healing will take some time, but you will heal."

"Keep telling me and maybe someday I'll believe it."

"I'll keep telling you. I'm relieved you're out of the hospital and the show's over."

"I owe you big for Morticia."

"You do what you gotta do. By the second night I was more tired than anything. Although I admit I made Letti and Kevin walk me to my car."

"Not Harlan?"

Rachel shook her head. "I haven't seen him since the shit with Leshawn went down. He may be avoiding me."

"Why? He was there that night. I thought you'd gotten back together."

"We haven't and we won't. Too many differences between us."

"You did what?"

"We broke it off. The morning you were raped Carrie came by the theater to tell me how it was. I tried to be nice, but I don't see things her way and I told her so. Harlan overheard and didn't appreciate my comments. He said I wasn't willing to see their point of view and I reminded him they hadn't tried to see mine. Although now I'm way more inclined to see theirs."

"Why now?"

Rachel took a breath. "I came this close to blowing Leshawn to smithereens." She held up her thumb and forefinger apart by a half of inch. "I wanted to kill his sorry ass so bad it wasn't funny. The only thing that stopped me was Daddy. He wouldn't have thought it was the right thing to do."

"No, he probably wouldn't. But then, if you had to do it to protect yourself and Harlan, it would've been a different story."

"I know. I didn't have to shoot him so I didn't. But I *wanted* to, Amy. Especially when I thought he was going to run off. Disappear and then come back and hurt you again. Like Carrie's boyfriend did to her. Abernathy threatened her kids like Leshawn threatened Granny." She turned to Amy. "Harlan was only twenty-one or twenty-two years old, when he killed Abernathy. He was just a kid himself, scared for his sister and certain the justice system wasn't going to save her. I have to ask myself. What would I have done at his age under the same circumstances? I barely stopped myself the other night. Would I have been able to if I'd been in Harlan's shoes?"

Amy looked at her for a minute. "I think you finally get it," she said softly. "Rachel, it's never been all black and white. It wasn't with Leshawn and it wasn't with the Burkes. Hell, I knew I was risking my life when I opened the door to Leshawn. But I was so damned scared for Granny I did it anyway. Carrie probably felt the same way.

"And it wasn't all black and white with Harlan, either," Amy went on. "He did what he felt he had to do. Do you finally understand?"

"Yeah, I do. Which makes me feel a little bad."

"Why, for crying out loud?"

"Daddy. I'm not sure he would've been too thrilled about me getting involved with a convicted felon, not that I let it stop me." She shrugged. "I'm thirty years old and he's been gone a long time."

"Yes, he has. I don't think he would've objected to you and Harlan. After all, he not only understood shades of gray, he lived them."

"Lived them? How so?"

"He married his black girlfriend whose father kept her and her mother on the side, knowing he was going to break his mother's heart and create a schism in the family. A man who saw things in black and white would never have married her, knowing what the consequences would be. As far as you getting involved with Harlan, it's certainly no worse or more scandalous than Daddy's romance with Mom."

"I never thought of it like that."

Amy's gaze held Rachel's. "What about you and Harlan? Is there any hope for the two of you getting back together?"

Rachel shook her head. "No. Our last fight was too rancorous," she said sadly. "We both said things we can't take back. He'll never be able to forgive me. It's over."

"Are you sure? Especially if you love him."

"I do love him. And I hurt for him. He sacrificed a lot to protect his sister. It changed the course of his life forever."

"Aside from the obvious, how?"

"His dream of being a baseball coach is toast, and he doesn't have a clue what he wants to do with himself. Plus, he thinks he's behind."

"Behind?"

"He would've had his degree and be well into his career. He took college courses in prison, but he's not even halfway near to getting a degree. It will be years before he has it."

He'll manage. I'm not worried. He's a fighter."

"It's not that easy."

"It's not easy for anybody. Sure, there are licenses and certifications he'll never be able to hold. But there's a lot of possibilities out there, lots of things he can do when he decides in what direction he wants to go. He needs to do some homework."

"And I need to make your lunch."

She fed Amy a bowl of soup and some cheese toast, and then insisted her sister take a nap. She wasn't expected back at the theater, so she sat at the computer and started searching, thinking about what Harlan was good at and what he liked to do and coming up with a list of links to some sites. She wasn't kidding herself. She wasn't doing this to get back in Harlan's good graces. It was over between them. But, she loved him, and he deserved a future. Despite his record, he was bright and talented, and if he knew what direction to aim, she had no doubt he would reach his goals and have the life he longed for. Maybe a nudge from her would help him aim in the right direction. A little homework was the least she could do to help him along a little.

She sighed and wiped away a tear. If things were different between them, she could do a lot more to help him achieve his dreams.

***

Rachel put the last of the dishes in the dishwasher. "You want a bowl of ice cream?" she asked as Amy eased herself up leaning on the kitchen table to get out of her chair.

"I'll pass. I don't have room for another bite. Nobody makes fried chicken like Granny."

"Hers has to be the best in the world."

"So what's *Abuela* sending over tomorrow?"

"Her *carne guisada*. Which she'll accompany with a stack of homemade flour tortillas. Don'cha love it when they start in with one of their competitions?"

Amy laughed. "One or the other of them has delivered something delicious every night since Mom brought them home. We're both gonna be rolling out of here if we don't watch it."

"Can't have that. Especially if you're gonna do *Memphis* next fall. Josh and I put it on the schedule this afternoon."

"Good." Amy said. "Gives me something to look forward to."

"It does. Things should be looking up for you by then."

"Things are already looking up. I have a long way to go before I get past what happened, but the shrink says I need to remind myself I have a lot going for me. I have a good job I'm going back to next week, and the theater. It's enough. It'll have to be enough. I'll be damned if I'm getting involved with men anymore."

"I know the feeling, considering the way things turned out with me and Harlan."

Amy wandered off and Rachel started the dishwasher. She flipped through the channels and was about to settle on a movie when the doorbell rang. She peeked out the window and spotted a familiar old truck in the driveway. Her heart skipped a beat and her breath hitched.

Harlan was here.

She peered out the window. He was standing on the porch, holding a gaily wrapped gift bag and looking at the front door doubtfully. She tamped down a spurt of excitement. Him being here might not mean anything. He might be dropping off a gift for Amy and nothing more. But he was here, which was more than she thought would ever happen.

She opened the door and looked at him as uncertainly as he was looking at her. "Come in," she said softly.

She opened the door a little wider and backed up to let him enter. A whiff of his soap and aftershave set off a wave of longing inside her. She missed him. She missed talking to him and laughing with him and making love to him on his futon. She'd dreamed of him more than once and woken up knowing she'd lost something precious and beautiful. Now he was here, and she couldn't help but think maybe he was not lost to her after all.

She could only hope.

She shut the front door. He looked around the room and whistled under his breath. "Is this the redo they were all talking about? Beautiful."

"They did a terrific job," Amy said as she came into the room. "It makes all the difference."

"I didn't find out until after the fact or I would have been here helping," he said. "How are you?"

"Slowly getting better. Rachel says the *American Idiot* sets are looking great."

Harlan smiled a little. "Definitely a different challenge than *Addams Family*. But I was able to repaint the big pieces and use them over."

"Super." She looked from Harlan to Rachel. "Good to see you. If you don't mind, I think I'm going to crawl back in the bed." She ducked out of the living room, leaving them alone.

"Her face is still bruised," he said quietly. "Her ribs still hurt. I can tell from the way she moves."

"The ribs are a matter of time. Her face is to the point she can cover it with makeup," Rachel said.

"I'm glad she's healing."

"She's going back to work on Monday. She'll want to look her best."

"She will. Here. This is for you." He thrust the package at her.

"Thanks." She took the gift bag. "Give me a minute and I'll get yours."

She ran to her bedroom and got his gift and the stack of printouts. "Come on out to the sunroom. With everything that's happened, we never got around to taking down the Christmas tree." She left the printouts on the kitchen counter. She'd give them to him on the way out.

He followed her, and she flicked on the lights and plugged in the tree. "It's still fresh," he commented.

"It's in a pot. It's going in *Abuela*'s front yard whenever one of us has time to plant it." She handed Harlan his gift and gestured to one of the chairs. "Go ahead."

"No. Ladies first."

She undid the ribbons and pulled out the tissue-wrapped gift gasping when she saw a gorgeous handbag. "It's beautiful," she breathed. She looked at the side zippers and giggled. "It's perfect. Thank you so much. My Sig Sauer will fit right in there."

"Did the police ever give you back the Ruger?"

"Nope. They said they need it for a while longer. That's okay. They can keep it as long as they need to if they're using it in building a case against Leshawn." She gestured to his package. "Your turn."

He ripped off the paper and opened the box. "Oh, wow. This is great." He gently fingered the leather jacket.

"Try it on."

He stood up and pulled on the jacket. "Perfect."

"Good. Your other one's too tight across the shoulders."

"It's from before. I've put on weight since I got it."

"Most people put on weight between twenty and thirty."

He explored the jacket, finding the inner and outer pockets before taking it off and laying it across the chair. He sat down and looked at her uncertainly. "I didn't come over just so I could bring your belated Christmas present. Could we talk?"

"Sure." She didn't know about him, but she had quite a bit she had to say.

"Okay. This isn't going to be easy to admit out loud." He paused and she made herself wait patiently. "The night with Leshawn in the parking lot. You could've shot him and didn't. When you turned him over to the cops, I realized something important." He stopped and swallowed. "Carrie and I, we fucked up royally. We should've done what you two did. She should've filed charges against him, reported the abuse, and testified against him when they needed her to. I should've let the law take care of him instead of killing him. I didn't have to. If we'd done things the way you and Amy did, I wouldn't have gone to prison. I could have gone to college and been teaching by now. I wouldn't be carrying around the shit pile of guilt I keep shoved under the rug."

"You never said anything about feeling guilty," she murmured.

"It's easy to deny feeling guilty when you've convinced yourself you did the right thing. Not so easy to deny when you're forced to admit you shouldn't've done it in the first place. Which ought to be good for a few visits to a shrink."

"A few, maybe. You have somebody? Amy likes the one she's using."

"I'll get the name. Anyway, it took me seeing how you and Amy handled things to realize how badly we messed up. I know you'll never understand, but I wanted you to know."

Rachel snorted. "What makes you think I'll never understand? I understand all too well."

His brows went up. "You do?"

"Absolutely. You have no idea how close I came to pulling the trigger." She held her thumb and forefinger apart. "This close. It was all I could do to hold him there until the cavalry arrived." She paused a minute. "I stood there thinking about Amy's black eye and busted ribs and split lips and whatever internal injuries he'd given her and the horror of rape itself, and I almost pulled the trigger."

His expression changed. Like he couldn't believe what he was hearing. "What stopped you?"

"What my father taught us. He would've expected us to let the legal system mete out justice. He also taught me to have faith in the system. If it hadn't been for his memory, I don't know what I would have done."

He looked at his hands. "He sure as hell wouldn't've approved of what I did. Probably wouldn't approve of me at all. No shades of gray for that guy."

"Honestly, I don't know how he would've felt about you. He understood shades of gray. Hell, you were only a kid. You'd lost your faith in the legal system and you really and truly believed the situation was hopeless. And Carrie was so beaten down she felt she couldn't stand up for herself. I get it now. I finally get it."

"I guess you could say the same for me. I finally get it."

They sat in silence for a few minutes. "What about Carrie?" she asked.

Harlan took a deep breath. "That was one miserable conversation. Let's say she and I are not on the same page yet. She still insists she couldn't do anything to stop Abernathy and she's furious at me for even suggesting otherwise. It may take her some time to come around."

"Time and counseling."

"If she'll go. But I didn't come here to talk about her. I came to talk about you and me."

Rachel smiled hesitantly. "Is there a you and me? After the fight we had I thought we were...through."

He reached out and took her hand. "Sure, we said things. But you know what? People who love each other can forgive most anything said in the heat of anger."

"People who love each other?"

"Yeah. I love you, Rachel. You love me too. I can feel it every time you touch me."

"I do love you. So much. But you don't seem so happy about it."

"I am. Believe me, I am." He picked up her hand and kissed it. "But there's not much I can do about it. Loving you, I mean."

"I'm not sure I agree. We can go over to your place and do plenty about it."

"Not what I meant." His expression was wistful as he looked at her. "I'd love to have a relationship with you. A real one, not lovers or friends with benefits. Something long term. Marriage, even. But I don't feel like it's right to ask you."

"Why not? Especially if I want it too."

"Even though I'm out of prison, I will always carry the stigma of being an ex-con. Plus, I have nothing to offer you. I'm at the same point in life most people are in their early twenties. I have about a third of a degree under my belt and it'll be years before I can finish college. Between working full time at jobs that don't pay too well and scraping together tuition money, it'll be years before I can support a family or take care of my half of the household expenses. You deserve better than spending years having to support my ass. Besides, I don't have a clue what I want to do. The only thing I ever wanted to do was coach baseball. I feel aimless, and I don't want that for you."

Rachel tilted her head. "I don't agree with everything you said, but you're right about one thing. Most people in their early twenties don't have a clue what they want to do. But guess what? A lot of thirty-year-olds don't either. I know a hell of a lot of people who have made midlife career changes. So that's not such a big deal."

"It is to me."

"Male pride rearing its ugly head."

"Probably. But jeez, honey, I don't have the first idea what I'd like to do. I've got enough hours I need to start thinking about a degree, but I'll be damned if I know what to get it in."

"You need a direction to go. Right? What do you like to do?"

"Besides making love to you?" He winked.

"Later." She leaned forward and gave him a quick lip touch. "Seriously, Harlan, what do you like? You're good at carpentry and your sets are something to die for. Do you like doing the work?"

"It's okay, but I don't love the construction stuff. I like designing them. I love that part. The actual building I do because it's the job. I know I'm good at it, but no. It's not my thing. I'd never tell Miguel, but the carpentry work I do for him is pure drudgery."

"Okay. So you like designing the sets but aren't wild about building them. Do you love Frank Lloyd Wright? Antony Gaudi? I.M. Pei? Or are Stuart Craig and David Korins your style?"

"Wright and Pei for sure. Gaudi's architecture's too old-fashioned. I love Stuart Craig's work on the Harry Potter movies, but have to admit Korins nailed the sets on *Hamilton*."

"You don't even know how far ahead of the pack you are." His brows went up. "How many people have a clue who those five men are? Damn few. But you not only know who they are, you're familiar with their work. Harlan, you might've been a wonderful coach, but clearly your interests lie in architecture and design. And your talent lies there as well. I had a feeling it did."

She jumped up and got the stack of printouts off the kitchen counter. "Here. Some stuff I got off the Internet the other day. I looked up universities offering architecture degrees, some of which are totally online. Now, to be honest, I don't know what your conviction will do to your ability to get licensed. I tried to look it up but don't speak legalese and had no idea what I was reading, but even without a license there's lot you can do with an architecture degree." She handed him another stack of printouts. "You haven't said anything about owning your own business, but every one of these building and remodeling companies is owned by an ex-con. You could design the kitchen or bathroom and pay carpenters to build it for you."

"Okaaay."

"If you were to go the set design route, I doubt you'd need a degree. But if you want one, there are plenty of design schools with online programs." She thrust the printouts of the architectural colleges into his hands.

He looked at her somewhat bemused. "So you think I'd be a good architect."

"I think you'd be a great architect. But it's not what I think. It's what you think that matters." She took a deep breath. "As far as your timeline and that male pride of yours, if you want to speed up the process, borrow the money like everyone else does. Take a full load and work part time."

"I thought financial aid wasn't available to convicted felons."

"Nope. It's unavailable only if you have a drug conviction. Everyone else is eligible. Even convicted murderers."

"You're shitting me."

"Nope. It's right there in black and white. You borrow the money, you knock out the degree, and speed up the timeline. Lots of people your age are still working on degrees. Hell, a lot of people are forty or more before they grab the brass ring. Jake Pierce is forty-five if he's a day and he's just now buying his clinic."

"It's a lot to think about. Me. An architect."

"I might be totally off base. You might be better off combining a business degree with your carpentry and set design skills. The point is you have a lot to offer me right now, and will have a lot more to offer in the future. That is, if you want to."

"Fuck yeah, I want to. I'll make something of myself, Rachel. I promise you. I'll be the man you deserve."

"And I'll be right there beside you every step of the way." She leaned over and captured his lips in a warm, loving kiss. He wrapped his strong arm around her and took the kiss deeper, and she felt his hopes and dreams pour into her.

They kissed for a long time before he pulled back and rested his forehead against hers. She smiled knowing down to her bones, they were going to be okay. More than okay. Happy. They'd build a life and a family, and he'd be her partner. Her friend, and her lifelong lover.

With their foreheads still touching and their lips a breath apart she whispered, "I have no doubt you'll make your life everything you want it to be."

"*Our* life, Rachel. It'll be our life. Together."

He was right. It would be.

EPILOGUE

Mike wiped his fingers on a napkin and finished the rest of his soda. The pizza had been a much-needed pick-me-up, and he was ready for whatever the crew did on their first night of Tech Week. He made a pit stop to the lobby restroom and was headed back to the auditorium when he spotted his brother-in-law Brian coming in the front door in the company of a young woman Mike had never seen before. He stared, riveted, as she and Brian stopped and spoke to an attractive couple who looked vaguely familiar. The woman was blonde and delicate, petite, and nearly ethereal in her beauty. But she seemed uncomfortable and wasn't interacting much with, speaking when spoken to but little else. He watched them for a minute before Brian looked in his direction and motioned him over. He wasn't sure he was in the mood to meet anyone, but this entire exercise was supposed to snap him out of his funk and meeting new people was part of it. He plastered on a smile he wasn't really feeling and crossed the lobby, his attention drawn to the blonde standing next to Brian.

They shook hands and Brian turned to the others. "I have someone I'd like you all to meet. This is Mike Werner, my brother-in-law. Mike, this is Letti and Kevin Summerset. You may have already met Letti." He turned to the blonde. "And this is Sasha Fontenot. These three are our leads in *Hello, Dolly*." He gestured toward the couple. "Letti's playing Dolly, at our benefactor Ernest Navarro's request, Kevin's playing Cornelius, and Sasha's playing Irene Molloy."

Mike quickly masked his surprise. He wouldn't have thought this quiet woman would be playing one of the leads.

Letti and Kevin murmured 'How do you do's and offered their hands. After a moment, Sasha shook hands as well, although she said nothing.

Letti looked at him curiously. "Jessica's brother-in-law?" Her smile slipped a bit.

"And Kinsey's father," Mike added. "Have you met my daughter Kinsey?"

Letti's smile warmed. "I have. She's precious."

A gorgeous dark-haired woman came in the front door and strode through the lobby, followed by an equally energetic woman with bouncing curls and a clipboard in her hands. "Uh-oh, the slave drivers are here," Brian said loudly, his eyes dancing with amusement. He turned to Mike. "Rachel's our director and Miranda's our production manager. Their entrance would be our cue to get down front for the rehearsal."

The three actors joined the rest of the cast in the front rows of the auditorium and Mike went back to the stage where the crew was moving set pieces into place to rehearse the first act. They'd scurry around during scene changes, rearranging the stage in the dark for each scene. He stood to one side of the stage and wiped his sweaty hands on his jeans. He reminded himself it was only a rehearsal and he wasn't in charge anyway. Besides, with the placement of each set piece and prop spiked onto the stage floor, there wasn't much room for error.

Rachel and Miranda gave thorough instructions to the cast and to the band upstairs in the balcony. An unsmiling Sasha listened intently. He still couldn't picture the withdrawn woman playing a lead. Maybe she'd landed the part based on her looks. For the rest of the actors, he hoped that wasn't the case.

The first scenes went well. Letti and Kevin as Dolly and Cornelius were impressive. Brian as Barnaby was properly young and innocent, and the young man playing Ambrose was knocking it out of the park. Then they rearranged the set for the first scene in Irene Malloy's shop. Sasha took her place on the stage, and before his eyes transformed from the unsmiling, withdrawn woman introduced to him in the lobby to the warm and engaging Irene Molloy, singing about how she would attract a man wearing a hat with ribbons down her back.

Mike was amazed.

Sasha could act. And sing. And hold her own with the other actors in the production.

Sasha finished her first scene and then another, retreating back into herself as she stepped out of character and becoming Irene during her scenes. It was the damnedest thing Mike had ever seen. The other actors did it too, of course. But the change wasn't as striking with them as it was with her.

He watched her, fascinated and more than a little attracted to her. He didn't know what to make of it. He hadn't been this drawn to a woman since he'd spotted Heather across a packed bar his senior year of college. He'd acted on the attraction to Heather right then and there. He'd like to tonight. But he was no longer a randy college kid. He was a thirty-six-year-old widower with a little girl to think of.

Still, he might speak to Sasha after rehearsal. Strike up a conversation, see if she would talk to him. It was worth a try.

They made it through the first act with no major glitches. They began the second act. As he and the rest of the crew placed the tables and chairs for the Harmonia Gardens restaurant, he glanced out at the auditorium and spotted his sister-in-law Jessica seated in the front row. He wondered why she hadn't come with Brian before he remembered something about her son Bobby and a birthday party.

The crew quickly set up the restaurant and the heavily male ensemble launched into the waiters' dance, complete with the obligatory spinning trays. They had almost finished the number when one of the younger dancers managed to get tangled up in a set chair and went crashing into the plywood set wall stage left. The piece came crashing toward the table and chairs where Sasha, Kevin, Brian, and Joyce, the girl playing Minnie were seated.

Acting on instinct, Mike tried to stop the fall of the huge set piece, throwing himself between the slab of plywood and the actors. But the piece was too heavy, and came down on top of him, knocking him on top of Sasha, who immediately began to kick and scream, pummeling him with her fists as he tried to get them out from under the piece. "Stop it," she screeched in his ear. "Get off me. Don't touch me/ *Leave me alone. Oh, noooooo!"*

Mike tried wiggling them both out from under the plywood, but the huge plank had them both trapped. "Damn it, lady, I'm trying," he ground out into her ear as he felt the piece being lifted off of them. One of the other crew members took him by the shoulders and lifted him from the terrified woman's body.

She scrambled out from under him and halfway across the stage before looking at him with sheer terror on her face. *What the fuck is her problem* he wondered as some of the other crew lifted the heavy piece off the other actors. Kevin and Brian got to their feet and pulled Joyce off the stage floor. All the while Sasha sat in the floor, trembling.

Rachel and Letti leapt to the stage and offered Sasha their hands, but she shook her head violently and struggled to get to her feet by herself.

Rachel called a fifteen-minute break and she and Miranda began an inspection of the set piece. The actors milled around backstage and the crew began righting the knocked over set.

Mike choked down the disappointment. So much for talking to her after the rehearsal. He shuddered at the close call. He'd dealt with one unstable woman in his life and had absolutely no desire to get tangled up with another.

The crew righted the tables and chairs and managed to get the huge piece put back in place. Mike watched as Rachel examined the set piece, talking animatedly on the phone to somebody named Harlan. Brian limped over and stood beside him. "Close call. It's a good thing you jumped in. Sasha could've been hurt badly."

Mike shrugged. "She wasn't exactly thankful. Jesus, you'd have thought I'd attacked her or something. God spare me from loony women."

Brian looked over Mike's shoulder and an odd expression crossed his face. *Uh-oh.* Mike glanced behind him. Sure enough, Sasha was standing a few feet behind him with a stricken look on her face. She'd heard every word he'd said. And from the pissed off expressions Letti and Jessica gave him, Sasha wasn't the only one.

ABOUT THE AUTHOR

The author of over forty romance novels, Emily Mims combined her writing career with a career in public education until leaving the classroom to write full time. The mother of two sons, she and her husband split their time between central Texas, eastern Tennessee, and overseas visiting their kids and grandchildren. For relaxation Emily plays the piano, organ, dulcimer, and ukulele for two different performing groups, and even sings a little. She says, "I love to write romances because I believe in them. Romance happened to me and it can happen to any woman—if she'll just let it."

Connect with Emily:

facebook: emily.mims.756

twitter: @emilymimsauthor

instagram: @mims_emily

website: emilymims.com

Boroughs
Publishing Group

www.BOROUGHSPUBLISHINGGROUP.com

If you enjoyed this book, please write a review. Our authors appreciate the feedback, and it helps future readers find books they love. We welcome your comments and invite you to send them to info@boroughspublishinggroup.com. Follow us on TikTok, Twitter, and Instagram, and be sure to sign up for our newsletter for surprises and new releases from your favorite authors.

Are you an aspiring writer? Check out www.boroughspublishinggroup.com/submit and see if we can help you make your dreams come true.

Love podcasts? Enjoy ours at www.boroughspublishinggroup.com/podcast